"Start t
truth."

She began sob

"I'm waiting," he growled you talking about? Whose is it? And where?"

Ivy sprang to her feet. "Get out of my way."

He grabbed her again, hauled her to her toes. "Answer me!"

Ivy looked up at him while the seconds seemed to turn to hours. Then she wrenched free of his hands.

"This baby," she said, laying a hand over her belly. "The one in my womb. I'm pregnant, Prince Damian. Pregnant—with your child."

THE BILLIONAIRES' BRIDES

by Sandra Marton

Pregnant by their princes...

Take three incredibly wealthy European princes
and match them with three beautiful, spirited women.
Add large helpings of intense emotion and passionate
attraction. Result: three unexpected pregnancies...
and three possible princesses—
if those princes have their way...

THE ITALIAN PRINCE'S PREGNANT BRIDE
Available in June

THE GREEK PRINCE'S CHOSEN WIFE
Available in September

THE SPANISH PRINCE'S VIRGIN BRIDE
Available in December

THE GREEK PRINCE'S CHOSEN WIFE

BY
SANDRA MARTON

MILLS & BOON®

First published in Great Britain 2007
Harlequin Mills & Boon Limited,
Eton House, 18-24 Paradise Road, Richmond, Surrey TW9 1SR

© Sandra Marton 2007

ISBN-13: 978 0 263 85344 5

Set in Times Roman 10 on 12¼ pt
01-0607-44776

Printed and bound in Spain
by Litografia Rosés, S.A., Barcelona

ROM
Pbk

THE GREEK
PRINCE'S
CHOSEN WIFE

My special thanks to Nadia-Anastasia Fahmi,
for her generous help with Greek idioms.
Any errors are, of course, entirely mine!

Sandra

CHAPTER ONE

DAMIAN was getting out of a taxi the first time he saw her.

He was in a black mood, something he'd grown accustomed to the last three months, a mood so dark he'd stopped noticing anything that even hinted at beauty.

But a man would have to be dead not to notice this woman.

Stunning, was his first thought. What he could see of her, anyway. Black wraparound sunglasses covered much of her face but her mouth was lusciously full with enough sexual promise to make a monk think of quitting the cloister.

Her hair was long. Silky-looking. A dichromatic mix of chestnut and gold that fell over her shoulders in a careless tumble.

And she was tall. Five-nine, five-ten with a model's bearing. A model's way of wearing her clothes, too, so that the expensive butterscotch leather blazer, slim-cut black trousers and high-heeled black boots made her look like she'd stepped straight out of the pages of *Vogue*.

A few short months ago, he'd have done more than

look. He'd have walked up to her, smiled, asked if she, too, were lunching at Portofino's…

But not today.

Not for the foreseeable future, he thought, his mouth thinning.

No matter what she looked like behind those dark glasses, he wasn't interested.

He swung away, handed the taxi driver a couple of bills. A driver behind his cab bleated his horn; Damian shot a look at the car, edged past it, stepped onto the curb…

And saw that the woman had taken off her sunglasses. She was looking straight at him, her gaze focused and steady.

She wasn't stunning.

She was spectacular.

Her face was a perfect oval, her cheekbones sharp as blades, her nose straight and aristocratic. Her eyes were incredible. Wide-set. Deep green. Heavily lashed.

And then there was that mouth. The things that mouth might do…

Hell!

Damian turned hard so quickly he couldn't believe it but then, he'd gone three months without a woman.

It was the longest he'd gone without sex since he'd been introduced to its mysteries the Christmas he was sixteen, when one of his father's many mistresses had seduced him.

The difference was that he'd been a boy then.

He was a man now. A man with cold hatred in his heart and no wish for a woman in his life, not yet, not even one this beautiful, this desirable…

"Hey, dude, this is New York! You think you own the sidewalk?"

Damian swung around, ready and eager for a fight, saw the speaker…and felt his tension drain away.

"Reyes," he said, smiling.

Lucas Reyes smiled in return. "In the flesh."

Damian's smile became a grin. He held out his hand, said, "Oh, what the hell," and pulled his old friend into a bear hug.

"It's good to see you."

"The same here." Lucas pulled back, his smile tilting. "Ready for lunch?"

"Aren't I always ready for a meal at Portofino's?"

"Yeah. Sure. I just—I meant…" Lucas cleared his throat. "You okay?"

"I'm fine."

"You should have called. By the time I read about the, ah, accident…"

Damian stiffened. "Forget it."

"That was one hell of a thing, man. To lose your fiancée…"

"I said, forget it."

"I didn't know her, but—"

"Lucas. I don't want to talk about it."

"If that's how you want it—"

"It's exactly how I want it," Damian said, with such cold surety that Lucas knew enough to back off.

"Okay," he said, forcing a smile. "In that case… I told Antonio to give us the back booth."

Damian forced a smile of his own. "Fine. Maybe they'll even have *Trippa alla Savoiarda* on the menu today."

Lucas shuddered. "What's the problem, Aristedes? Pasta's not good enough for you?"

"Tripe's delicious," Damian said and just that easily,

they fell into the banter that comes with old friendships.

"Just like old times," Lucas said.

Nothing would ever be like old times again, Damian thought, but he grinned, too, and let it go at that.

The back booth was as comfortable as ever and the tripe was on the menu. Damian didn't order it; he never had. Tripe made him shudder the same as Lucas.

The teasing was just part of their relationship.

Still, after they'd ordered, after his double vodka on the rocks and Lucas's whiskey, straight up, had arrived, he and Lucas both fell silent.

"So," Lucas finally said, "what's new?"

Damian shrugged. "Nothing much. How about you?"

"Oh, you know. I was in Tahiti last week, checking out a property on the beach…"

"A tough life," Damian said, and smiled.

"Yeah, well, somebody has to do it."

More silence. Lucas cleared his throat.

"I saw Nicolo and Aimee over the weekend. At that dinner party. Everyone was sorry you didn't come."

"How are they?" Damian said, deliberately ignoring the comment.

"Great. The baby's great, too."

Silence again. Lucas took a sip of his whiskey.

"Nicolo said he'd tried to call you but—"

"Yes. I got his messages."

"I tried, too. For weeks. I'm glad you finally picked up the phone yesterday."

"Right," Damian said as if he meant it, but he didn't. Ten minutes in and he already regretted taking Lucas's call and agreeing to meet him.

At least mistakes like this one could be remedied, he thought, and glanced at his watch.

"The only thing is," he said, "something's come up. I'm not sure I can stay for lunch. I'll try, but—"

"Bull."

Damian looked up. "What?"

"You heard me, Aristedes. I said, 'bull.' Nothing's come up. You just want a way to get out of what's coming."

"And that would be…?"

"A question."

"Ask it, then."

"Why didn't you tell Nicolo or me when it happened? Why let us hear about it through those damned scandal sheets?"

"That's two questions," Damian said evenly.

"Yeah, well, here's a third. Why didn't you lean on us? There wasn't a damned reason for you to go through all of that alone."

"All of what?"

"Give me a break, Damian. You know all of what. Hell, man, losing the woman you love…"

"You make it sound as if I misplaced her," Damian said, his voice flat and cold.

"You know I didn't mean it that way. It's just that Nicolo and I talked about it and—"

"Is that all you and Barbieri have to keep you busy? Gossip like a pair of old women?"

He saw Lucas's eyes narrow. Why wouldn't they? Damian knew he was tossing Lucas's concern in his teeth but to hell with that. The last thing he wanted was sympathy.

"We care about you," Lucas said quietly. "We just want to help."

Damian gave a mirthless laugh. He saw Lucas blink and he leaned toward him across the table.

"Help me through my sorrow, you mean?"

"Yes, damn it. Why not?"

"The only way you could help me," Damian said, very softly, "would be by bringing Kay back."

"I know. I understand. I—"

"No," he said coldly, "you do not know. You do not understand. I don't want her back to ease my sorrow, Lucas."

"Then, what—"

"I want her back so I can tell her I know exactly what she was. That she was a—"

The men fell silent as the waiter appeared with Damian's second double vodka. He put it down and looked at Lucas, who took less than a second to nod in assent.

"Another whiskey," he said. "Make it a double."

They waited until the drink had been served. Then Lucas leaned forward.

"Look," he said softly, "I know you're bitter. Who wouldn't be? Your fiancée, pregnant. A drunk driver, a narrow road…" He lifted his glass, took a long swallow. "It's got to be rough. I mean, I didn't know Kay, but—"

"That's the second time you said that. And you're right, you didn't know her."

"Well, you fell in love, proposed to her in a hurry. And—"

"Love had nothing to do with it."

Lucas stared at him. "No?"

Damian stared back. Maybe it was the vodka. Maybe it was the way his old friend was looking at him. Maybe it was the sudden, unbidden memory of the woman outside the restaurant, how there'd been a time he'd have wanted her and not despised himself for it.

Who knew the reason? All he was sure of was that he was tired of keeping the truth buried inside.

"I didn't propose. She moved in with me, here in New York."

"Yeah, well—"

"She was pregnant," Damian said flatly. "Then she lost the baby. Or so she said."

"What do you mean?"

"She'd never been pregnant." Damian's jaw tightened. "The baby was a lie."

Lucas's face paled. "Hell, man. She scammed you!"

If there'd been one touch of pity in those words, Damian would have gotten to his feet and walked out. But there wasn't. All he heard in Lucas's voice was shock, indignation and a welcome hint of anger.

Suddenly the muted sounds of voices and laughter, the delicate clink of glasses and cutlery were almost painfully obtrusive. Damian stood, dropped several bills on the table and looked at Lucas.

"I bought a condo. It's just a few blocks from here."

Lucas was on his feet before Damian finished speaking.

"Let's go."

And right then, right there, for the first time since it had all started, Damian began to think he'd be okay.

A couple of hours later, the men sat facing each other in the living room of Damian's fifteen-room duplex. Vodka and whiskey had given way to a pot of strong black coffee.

The view through three surrounding walls of glass was magnificent but neither man paid it any attention. The only view that mattered was the one Damian was providing into the soul of a scheming woman.

"So," Lucas said quietly, "you'd been with her for some time."

Damian nodded. "Whenever I was in New York."

"And then you tried to break things off."

"Yes. She was beautiful. Sexy as hell. But the longer I knew her… I suppose it sounds crazy but it was as if she'd been wearing a mask and now she was letting it slip."

"That's not crazy at all," Lucas said grimly. "There are women out there who'll do anything to land a man with money."

"She began to show a side I hadn't seen before. She cared only for possessions, treated people as if they were dirt. Cabbies, waitresses…" Damian drank some of his coffee. "I wanted out."

"Who wouldn't?"

"I thought about just not calling her anymore, but I knew that would be wrong. Telling her things were over seemed the decent thing to do. So I called, asked her to dinner." His face turned grim and he rose to his feet, walked to one of the glass walls and stared out over the city. "I got one sentence out and she began to cry. And she told me she was pregnant with my baby."

"You believed her?"

Damian swung around and looked at Lucas. "She'd been my mistress for a couple of months, Lucas. You'd have done the same."

Lucas sighed and got to his feet. "You're right." He paused. "So, what did you do?"

"I said I'd support her and the baby. *She* said if I really cared about the baby in her womb, I would ask her to move in with me."

"Dear God, man—"

"Yes. I know. But she was carrying my child. At least, that's what I believed."

Lucas sighed again. "Of course."

"It was a nightmare," Damian said, shuddering. "I guess she thought it was safe to drop the last of her act. She treated my staff like slaves, ran up a six figure charge at Tiffany…" His jaw knotted. "I didn't want anything to do with her."

"No sex?" Lucas asked bluntly.

"None. I couldn't imagine why I'd slept with her in the first place. She thought I'd lost interest because she was pregnant." He grimaced. "She began talking about how different things would be, if she weren't…" Damian started toward the table that held the coffee service. Halfway there, he muttered something in Greek, veered past it and went instead to a teak cabinet on the wall. "What are you drinking?"

"Whatever you're pouring."

The answer brought a semblance of a smile to Damian's lips. He poured healthy amounts of Courvoisier into a pair of crystal brandy snifters and held one out. The men drank. Then Damian spoke again.

"A couple of weeks later, she told me she'd miscarried. I felt—I don't know what I felt. Upset, at the loss of the baby. I mean, by then I'd come to think of it as a baby, you know? Not a collection of cells." He shook his head. "Once I got past that, what I felt, to be honest, was relief. Now we could end the relationship."

"Except, she didn't want to end it."

Damian gave a bitter laugh. "You're smarter than I was. She became hysterical. She said I'd made promises, begged her to spend her life with me."

"But you hadn't."

"Damned right, I hadn't. The only thing that had drawn us together was the baby. Right?"

"Right," Lucas said, although he was starting to realize he didn't have to say anything. The flood gates had opened.

"She seemed to plummet into depression. Stayed in bed all day. Wouldn't eat. Went to her obstetrician—at least she said she'd gone to her obstetrician—and told me he'd advised her to get pregnant again."

"But—"

"Exactly. I didn't want a child, not with her. I wanted out." Damian took another swallow of brandy. "She begged me to reconsider. She'd come into my room in the middle of the night—"

"You had separate rooms?"

A cold light flared in Damian's eyes. "From the start."

"Sure, sure. Sorry. You were saying—"

"She was good at what she did. I have to give her that. Most nights, I turned her away but once…" A muscle knotted in his jaw. "I'm not proud of it."

"Man, don't beat yourself up. If she seduced you—"

"I used a condom. It made her crazy. 'I want your baby,' she said. "And then—"

Damian fell silent. Lucas leaned forward. "And then?"

"And then," Damian said, after a deep breath and a

long exhalation, "then she told me she'd conceived. That her doctor had confirmed it."

"But the condom—"

"It broke, she said, when she—when she took it off me—" He cleared his throat. "Hell, why would I question it? The damned things do break. We all know that."

"So—so she was pregnant again."

"No," Damian said flatly. "She wasn't pregnant. Oh, she went through all the motions. Morning sickness, ice cream and pickles in the middle of the night. But she wasn't pregnant." His voice roughened. "She never had been. Not then, not ever."

"Damian. You can't be sure of—"

"She wanted my name. My money." Damian gave a choked laugh. "Even my title, the 'Prince' thing you and I both know is nothing but outdated crap. She wanted everything." He drew a deep breath, then blew it out. "And she lied about carrying my child to get it."

"When did you find out?"

"When she died," Damian said flatly. He drained his glass and refilled it. "I was in Athens on business. I phoned her every night to see how the pregnancy was going. Later, I found out she'd taken a lover and she'd been with him all the time I was gone."

"Hell," Lucas said softly.

"They were on Long Island. A narrow, twisting road on the Sound along the North Shore. He was driving, both of them high on booze and cocaine. The car went over a guardrail. Neither of them survived." Damian looked up from his glass, his eyes bleak. "You talked about grief before, Lucas. Well, I *did* grieve then, not for her but for my unborn child…until I was going through Kay's papers, tying up loose ends, and found an article she'd clipped from some magazine, all about the symptoms of pregnancy."

"That still doesn't mean—"

"I went to see her doctor. He confirmed it. She had never been pregnant. Not the first time. Not the second. It was all a fraud."

The two friends sat in silence while the sun dipped below the horizon. Finally Lucas cleared his throat.

"I wish I could think of something clever to say."

Damian smiled. "You got me to talk. You can't imagine how much good that's done. I'd been keeping everything bottled inside."

"I have an idea. That club of mine. Remember? I'm meeting there with someone interested in buying me out."

"So soon?"

"You know how it is in New York. Today's hotspot is tomorrow's trash." Lucas glanced at his watch. "Come downtown with me, have a drink while I talk a little business and then we'll go out." He grinned. "Dinner at that place on Spring Street. A pair of bachelors on the town, like the old days."

"Thank you, my friend, but I wouldn't be very good company tonight."

"Of course you would. And we won't be alone for long." Another quick grin. "Before you know it, there'll be a couple of beautiful women hovering over us."

"I've sworn off women for a while."

"I can understand that but—"

"It's what I need to do right now."

"You sure?"

Inexplicably an image of the woman with green eyes

and sun-streaked hair flashed before Damian's eyes. He hadn't wanted to notice her, certainly didn't want to remember her…

"Yes," he said briskly, "I'm positive."

"You know what they say about getting back on the horse that threw you," Lucas said with a little smile.

"I told Nicolo almost the same thing a year ago, the night he met Aimee."

"And?"

"And," Damian said, "it was good advice for him, but not for me. This is different."

Lucas's smile faded. "You're right. Well, let me just call this guy I'm supposed to meet—"

"No, don't do that. I'd like to be alone tonight. Just do a little thinking, start putting this thing behind me."

Lucas cocked his head. "It's no big deal, Damian. I can meet him tomorrow."

"I appreciate it but, honestly, I feel a lot better now that we talked." Damian held out his hand. "Go have your meeting. And, Lucas— Thank you."

"*Para nada,*" Lucas said, smiling. "I'll call you tomorrow, yes? Maybe we can have dinner together."

"I wish I could but I'm flying back to Minos in the morning." Damian gripped Lucas's shoulder. "Take care of yourself, *filos mou.*"

"You do the same." Lucas frowned. Damian looked better than he had a few hours ago but there was still a haunted look in his eyes. "I wish you'd change your mind about tonight. Forget what I said about women. We could go to the gym. Lift some weights. Run the track."

"You really think it would make me feel better to beat you again?"

"You beat me once, a thousand years ago at Yale."

"A triviality."

The men chuckled. Damian slung his arm around Lucas's neck as they walked slowly to the door. "Don't worry about me, Reyes. I'm going to take a long shower, pour myself another brandy and then, thanks to you, I'm going to have the first real night's sleep I've had in months."

The friends shook hands. Then Damian closed the door after Lucas, leaned back against it and let his smile slip away.

He'd told Lucas the truth. He did feel better. For three months, ever since Kay's death, he'd avoided his friends, his acquaintances; he'd dedicated every waking minute to business in hopes he could rid himself of his anger.

What was the point in being angry at a dead woman?

Or in being angry at himself, for having let her scam him?

"No point," Damian muttered as he climbed the stairs to his bedroom. "No point at all."

Kay had made a fool of him. So what? Men survived worse. And if, in the deepest recesses of his soul he somehow mourned the loss of a child that had never existed, a child he'd never known he even wanted, well, that could be dealt with, too.

He was thirty-one years old. Maybe it was time to settle down. Marry. Have a family.

Thee mou, was he insane?

You couldn't marry, have kids without a wife. And there wasn't a way in hell he was going to take a wife anytime soon. What he needed was just the opposite of settling down.

Lucas had it right.

The best cure for what ailed him would be losing himself in a woman. A soft, willing body. An eager mouth. A woman without a hidden agenda, without any plans beyond pleasure…

There it was. That same image again. The green-eyed woman with the sun-streaked hair. Hell, what a chance he'd missed! She'd looked right at him and even then, trapped in a black mood, he'd known what that look meant.

The lady had been interested.

The flat truth was, women generally were.

He'd been interested, too—or he would have been, if he hadn't been so damned busy wallowing in self-pity. Because, hell, that's what this was. Anger, sure, but with a healthy dollop of Poor Me mixed in.

He'd had enough of it to last a lifetime.

He'd call Lucas. Tell him his plans for the night sounded good after all. Dinner, drinks, a couple of beautiful women and so what if they didn't have green eyes, sun-streaked hair…

The doorbell rang.

Damian's brows lifted. A private elevator was the sole access to his apartment. Nobody could enter it without the doorman's approval and that approval had to come straight from Damian himself.

Unless…

He grinned. "Lucas," he said, as he went quickly down the stairs. His friend had reached the lobby, turned around and come right back.

Damian reached the double doors. "Reyes," he said happily as he flung them open, "when did you take up mind-reading? I was just going to call you—"

But it wasn't Lucas in the marble foyer.

It was the woman. The one he'd seen outside Portofino's.

The green-eyed beauty he hadn't been able to get out of his head.

CHAPTER TWO

OH, WHAT a joy to see!

Damian Aristedes's handsome jaw dropped halfway to the ground. Seeing that was the first really good thing that had happened to Ivy in a while.

Obviously his highness wasn't accustomed to having his life disrupted by unwanted surprises.

Damian's unflappable, Kay had said.

Well, okay. She hadn't said it exactly that way. *Nobody can get to him,* was probably more accurate.

Not true, Ivy thought. Just look at the man now.

"Who are you? What are you doing here?"

She didn't answer. The pleasure of catching him off guard was wearing off. She'd prepared for this moment but the reality was terrifying. Her heart was hammering so hard she was half afraid he could hear it.

"You were outside Portofino's today."

He was gaining control of himself. His voice had taken on authority; his pale gray eyes had narrowed.

"Are you a reporter for one of those damned tabloids? I don't give interviews."

He really didn't know who she was. She'd wondered about that, whether Kay had ever shown him a photo or pointed out her picture in a magazine, but she'd pretty much squelched that possibility at the restaurant, where she'd followed him from his Fifty-Seventh Street office.

He'd looked at her, but only the way most men looked at her. With interest, avarice—the kind of hunger she despised, the kind that said she was a plaything and they wanted a new toy.

Although, when this man had looked at her today, just for a second, surely no more than that, she'd felt— she'd felt—

What?

She'd seemed to lose her equilibrium. She was glad someone had joined him because she knew better than to confront him with another person around.

This discussion had to be private.

As for that loss of equilibrium or whatever it was, it only proved how dangerous Damian Aristedes was.

That he'd been able to mesmerize Kay was easy to understand. Kay had always been a fool for men.

That he'd had an effect on Ivy, even for a heartbeat, only convinced her she'd figured him right.

The prince of all he surveyed was a sleek jungle cat, constantly on the prowl. A beautiful predator. Too bad he had no soul, no heart, no—

"Are you deaf, woman? Who are you? What do you want? And how in hell did you get up here?"

He'd taken a couple of steps forward, just enough to invade her space. No question it was a subtle form of intimidation. It might have worked, too—despite her height, he was big enough so that she had to tilt her head back to meet his eyes—but Ivy was not a stranger to intimidation.

Growing up, she'd been bullied by experts. It could only hurt if you gave in to it.

"Three questions," she said briskly. "Did you want them answered in order, or am I free to pick and choose?"

He moved quickly, grasped her wrist and forced her arm behind her back. It hurt; his grip was strong, his hands hard. She hadn't expected a show of physical strength from a pampered aristocrat but she didn't flinch.

"Take your hand off me."

"It'll take me one second to phone for the police and tell them there's an intruder in my home. Is that what you want?"

"You're the one who won't want the police involved in this, Your Highness."

His gray eyes focused on hers. "Because?"

Now, Ivy thought, and took a steadying breath.

"My name is Ivy."

Nothing. Not even a flicker of interest.

"Ivy Madison," she added, as if that would make the difference.

He didn't even blink. He was either a damned good actor or— A tingle of alarm danced over her skin.

"You are—you are Damian Aristedes?"

He smiled thinly. "A little late to ask but yes, that's who I am."

"Then—then surely, you recognize my name…"

"I do not."

"I'm Kay's sister. Her stepsister."

That got a reaction. His eyes turned cold. He let go of her wrist, or maybe it made more sense to say he dropped it. She half expected him to wipe his hand on his trousers. Instead he stepped back.

"Here to pay a condolence call three months late?"

"I'd have thought you'd have been the one to call me."

He laughed, although the sound he made had no mirth to it.

"Now, why in hell would I do that? For starters, I never knew Kay had a sister." He paused. "That is, if you really are her sister."

"What are you talking about? Certainly I'm her sister. And, of course you know about me."

The woman who claimed to be Kay's sister spoke with authority. Not that Damian believed she really was who she claimed to be.

At the very least she was up to no good. Why approach him this way instead of phoning or e-mailing? What the hell was going on here?

Only one way to find out, Damian thought, and reached for his cell phone, lying on the marble-topped table beside the door.

"What are you doing?"

"Calling your bluff. You won't answer my questions? Fine. You can tell your story to the cops."

"You'd better think twice before you pick up that phone, Mr. Aristedes."

His intruder had started out full of conviction, like a poker player sure of a winning hand, but that had changed. Her voice had gone from strong to shaken; those green eyes—so green he wondered if she were wearing contact lenses—had gone wide.

A scam, he thought coldly. She was trying to set him up for something. The only question was, what?

"Prince," he said, surprising himself with the use of his title. Generally he asked people to call him by his first or last name, not by his honorific, but if it took royal arrogance to shake his intruder's self-control, he'd use it. "It's Prince Damian. And I'll give you one second to start talking. How did you get up here?"

"You mean, how did I bypass the lobby stormtroopers?"

She was trying to regain control. Damned if he'd let it happen. Damian put down the phone, angled toward her and invaded her space again so that she not only stepped back, she stepped into the corner.

No way out, except past him.

"Don't play with me, lady. I want straight answers."

She caught a bit of her lower lip between her teeth, worried it for a second before releasing it and quickly touching the tip of her tongue to the flesh she'd gnawed.

Damian's belly clenched. Lucas had it right. He'd been too long without a woman.

"A delivery boy at the service entrance held the door for me." She smiled thinly. "He was very courteous. Then I used the fire stairs."

"If you're Kay's sister, why didn't you simply ask the doorman to announce you?"

"I waited all this time to hear from you but nothing happened. Telling your doorman I wanted to see you didn't strike me as useful."

"Let me see some ID."

"What?"

"Identification. Something that says you're who you claim to be."

"I don't know why Kay loved you," Ivy said bitterly.

Damian decided it was the better part of valor not to answer that. Instead he watched in silence as she dug through the bag slung over one shoulder, took out a wallet and opened it.

"Here. My driver's license. Satisfied?"

Not satisfied, just more puzzled. The license said she was Ivy Madison, age twenty-seven, with an address in Chelsea. And the photo checked out. It was the woman standing before him. Not even the bored Motor Vehicle clerks and their soulless machines had been able to snap a picture that dimmed her looks.

Damian looked up.

"This doesn't make you Kay's sister."

Without a word, she dug into her purse again, took out a business-card size folder and flipped it open. The photo inside was obviously years old but there was no mistaking the faces of the two women looking at the camera.

"All right. What if you are Kay's sister. Why are you here?"

Ivy stared at him. "You can't be serious!"

He was…and then, with breathtaking speed, things started to fall into place.

The sisters didn't resemble each other, but that didn't mean the apple had fallen far from the tree.

"Let me save you some time," Damian said coolly. "Your sister didn't leave any money."

Those bright green eyes flashed with defiance. "I'm not here for money."

"There's no jewelry, either. No spoils of war. I donated everything I'd given her to charity."

"I don't care about that, either."

"Really?" He folded his arms. "You mean, I haven't ruined your hopes for a big score?"

Her eyes filled with tears.

Indeed, Damian thought grimly, that was exactly what he'd done.

"You—you egotistical, self-aggrandizing, aristocratic pig," she hissed, her voice shaking. "You haven't spoiled anything except for yourself. And believe me, Prince or Mr. or whatever name you want, you'll never, ever know what you missed!"

It was an emotional little speech and he could see she was determined to end it on a high note by shoving past him and striding to the door.

There was every reason to let her go.

If she was willing to give up so easily and disappear from his life as quickly as she'd entered it, who was he to stop her?

Logic told him to move aside.

To hell with logic.

Damian shifted his weight to keep her trapped in the corner. She called him another name, not nearly as creative as the last, put her arms out straight and tried to push him away.

He laughed, caught both her wrists and trapped her hands against the hard wall of his chest. Anger and defiance stained her cheeks with crimson.

"Damn it, let go!"

"Why, sweetheart," he purred, "I don't understand. How come you're so eager to leave when you were so eager to see me?"

She kicked him in the shin with one of her high heeled boots. It hurt, but he'd be damned if he let her know that. Instead he dragged her closer until she was pressed against him.

He told himself it was only to keep her from gouging his shin to the bone.

And that there was no reason, either, for the hot fist of lust that knotted in his groin as he looked down into her flushed face.

Her eyes were wild. Her hair was a torrent of spun gold. Her lips were trembling. Trembling, and full, and delicately parted, and all at once, all at once, Damian understood why she was here.

What a thickheaded idiot he was!

Kay had obviously told Ivy about him. That he had money, a title, an eye for beautiful women.

And now Kay was gone but Ivy—Ivy was very much alive.

Incredibly alive.

His gaze dropped to her mouth again. "What a fool you must think me," he said softly. "Of course I know why you're here."

Her eyes lit. Her mouth curved in a smile. "Thank God," she said shakily. "For a while there, I thought—"

Damian silenced her in midsentence. He thrust his hands into her hair, lifted her face to his and kissed her.

She cried out against his mouth. Slammed her fists against his chest. A nice touch, he thought with a coldness that belied his rising libido. She'd come to audition as her sister's replacement. Well, he'd give her a tryout, all right. Kiss her, show her she had no effect on him and then send her packing.

Except, it wasn't happening that way.

Maybe he really had been without a woman for too long.

Maybe his emotions were out of control.

Sex, desire—neither asks for reason, only satiation and completion. He wanted this. The heat building inside him like a flash-fire in dry brush. The deep, hungry kiss.

The woman struggling for freedom in his arms.

She was pretending. He knew that. It was all part of the act. He nipped at her bottom lip; she gave a little cry and he slid his tongue into her mouth, tasted her sweetness, caught the little sound she made and kissed her again and again until she whimpered, lifted herself to him, flattened her hands against his chest…

Thee mou!

Damian jerked away. The woman stumbled back. Her eyes flew open, the pupils so enormous they'd all but consumed the green of her irises.

What the hell was he doing? She was just like Kay. A siren, luring a man with sex—

Her hand flew through the air and slammed against his jaw.

"You bastard," she said in a hoarse whisper. "You evil, horrible son of a bitch!"

"Don't bother with the theatrics," he snarled. "Or I'll call you some names of my own."

"I don't understand why Kay loved you!"

"Your sister never loved anything that didn't have a price tag on it. Now, go on. Get the hell out before I change my mind and call the police."

"She loved you enough to let you talk her into having this baby!"

Damian had swung away. Now he turned around and faced Ivy Madison.

"What are you talking about?"

"You know damned well what I'm talking about! She lost the first baby and instead of offering her any comfort and compassion, you told her to get out because she couldn't give you an heir."

Could a woman's lies actually leave a man speechless? Damian opened his mouth, then shut it again while he tried to make sense of what Ivy Madison had just said.

"You would have tossed away the woman who loved

you, who adored you, just because she couldn't give you a child. So my sister said she'd give you a baby, no matter what it took, even after the doctors said she couldn't run the risk of pregnancy!"

"Wait a minute. Just wait one damned minute—"

Ivy stared at him, emerald eyes bright against the pallor of her skin.

"You used her love for you to try to get your own way and you didn't care what it did to her, what happened to her—"

Damian was on her in two strides, hands gripping her shoulders, fingers biting into her flesh, lifting her to her toes so that their faces were inches apart.

"Get out," he said in a low, dangerous voice. "Do you hear me? Get out of my home and my life or I'll have you arrested. And if you think you'll walk away after a couple of hours in jail, think again. My attorneys will see to it that you stay in prison for the next hundred years."

It was an empty threat. What could he charge her with besides being a world-class liar? He knew that. What counted was that she didn't.

But it didn't stop her.

"Kay was in love with you."

"I just told you what Kay loved. You have five seconds, Miss Madison. One. Two—"

"She found a way to have your child. You were happy to go along with it but now, you refuse to acknowledge that—"

"Goodbye, Miss Madison."

Damian spun Ivy toward the door. He put his hand in the small of her back, gave her a little push and she stumbled toward the elevator.

"I'm going to call down to the lobby. If the doorman

doesn't see you stepping out of this car in the next couple of minutes, the cops will be waiting."

"You can't do this!"

"Just watch me."

The elevator door opened. Damian curled his fingers around her elbow and quick-marched her inside.

Tears were streaming down her face.

She was as good at crying on demand as Kay had been, he thought dispassionately, though Kay had never quite mastered the art. Her face would get red, her skin blotchy but despite all that, her nose never ran.

Ivy's eyes were cloudy with tears. Her skin was the color of cream. And her nose—damn it, her nose was leaking.

A nice touch of authenticity, Damian told himself as he stepped from the car and the door began to close.

"I was a fool to come here."

Damian grabbed the door. Her words were slurred. Another nice touch, he thought, and offered a wicked smile.

"Didn't work out quite the way you'd planned it, did it?"

"I should have known. All these months, no call from you…"

"I'm every bit the son of a bitch you imagined I'd be," he said, smiling again.

"I tried to tell Kay it was a bad idea, but she wouldn't listen."

"I'll bet. Two con artists discussing how to handle a sucker. Must have been one hell of a conversation."

She brushed the back of her hand over her eyes but, more credit to her acting skills, the tears kept coming.

"Just be sure of one thing, Prince Aristedes."

"It's Prince Damian," he said coolly. "If you're going to try to work royalty, you should use the proper form of address."

"Don't think you can change your mind after the baby's born."

"I wouldn't dream of…" He jerked back. "What baby?"

"Because I won't let you near this child. I don't give a damn how many lawyers you turn loose on me!"

Damian stared at her. He'd let go of the elevator door and it was starting to close again. He moved fast and forced it open.

"What baby?" he demanded.

"You know damned well what baby! Mine. I mean, Kay's." Ivy's chin lifted. "Kay's—and yours."

The earth gave a sickening tilt under his feet. There was a baby? No. There couldn't be. Kay had never really been pregnant. Her doctor had told him so…

"You're a vicious little liar!"

"Fine. Stay with that idea. I told you, I won't let my baby—Kay's baby—near a son of a bitch like—"

She let out a shriek as he dragged her from the elevator, marched her into his apartment and all but threw her into a chair.

"What the hell are you talking about?" He stood over her, feet apart, arms folded, eyes blazing with anger. "Start talking, and it better be the truth."

She began sobbing. He didn't give a damn.

"I'm waiting," he growled. "What baby are you talking about? Whose is it? And where?"

Ivy sprang to her feet. "Get out of my way."

He grabbed her again, hauled her to her toes.

"Answer me, goddamn it!"

Ivy looked up at him while the seconds seemed to turn to hours. Then she wrenched free of his hands.

This baby," she said, laying a hand over her belly. "The one in my womb. I'm pregnant, Prince Damian. Pregnant—with your child."

CHAPTER THREE

PREGNANT?

Pregnant, with his child?

Damian's brain reeled.

Thee mou, a man didn't want to hear that accusation from a woman he didn't love once in a lifetime, let alone twice...

And then his sanity returned.

This woman, Ivy, might well be pregnant but it didn't have a damned thing to do with him. Not unless science had come up with a way a man could have sex with a woman without ever seeing her or touching her.

She was looking at him, defiance stamped in every feature. What was she waiting for? Was he supposed to blink, fall down, clap his hand to his forehead?

The only thing he felt like doing was tossing her over his shoulder and throwing her out. But first—but first—

Damian snorted. Snorted again and then, to hell with it, burst out laughing.

Ivy Madison gave him a killing look.

"How can you laugh at this?" she demanded.

That only made him laugh harder.

He'd heard some really creative tall tales in his life. His father had been especially adept at telling them as he took his company to the edge of ruin but nothing, *nothing* topped this one.

It was funny.

It was infuriating.

Did she take him for a complete fool? Her sister had. Yes, but at least he'd had sex with the sister. There'd been a basis—shaky, but a basis—for Kay claiming she was pregnant.

Hell, the hours the two women must have spent talking about what a sucker he was, how easily he could be taken in by a beautiful face.

"Perhaps you'd like to share what's so damned amusing, Prince Damian?"

Amusing? Damian's laughter faded. "Actually," he said, "I'm insulted."

She blinked. "Insulted?"

"That you'd come up with such a pathetic lie." He tucked his hands in his trouser pockets and sighed dramatically. "You have to have sex with a man before he can impregnate you, Miss Madison, and you and I…"

Suddenly he knew where this was heading. He'd heard of scams like it before.

A beautiful woman chooses a man who's rich. Well-known. A man whose name would garner space in the tabloids.

When the time is right, she confronts him, tells him they met at a party, on a yacht—there were dozens of places they could have stumbled across each other.

That established, she drops the bomb.

She's pregnant. He's responsible. When he says *That's impossible, I never saw you before in my life*, she starts to cry. He was drinking that night, she says. He seduced her, she says. Doesn't he remember?

Because she does.

Every touch. Every sigh. Every nuance of their encounter is seared in her memory, and if he doesn't want it all over the scandal sheets, he'll Do The Right Thing.

He'll give her a fat sum of money to help her. Nothing like a bribe, of course. Just money to get her through a bad time.

Some men would give in without much of a fight, even if they could disprove the story. They'd do whatever it took just to avoid publicity.

Damian's jaw tightened.

Oh, yes. That was how this was supposed to go down... Except, it wouldn't. His beautiful scam artist was about to learn she couldn't draw him into that kind of trap.

He'd already been the victim of one Madison sister. He'd be damned if he'd be the victim of the second sister, too.

Damian looked up. The woman had not moved. She stood her ground, shoulders squared, head up, eyes glittering with defiance.

God, she was magnificent! Anyone walking in and seeing her would be sure she was a brave Amazon, overmatched but prepared to fight to her last breath.

Too bad there wasn't an audience. There was only him, and he wasn't buying the act.

Damian smiled. Slowly he brought his hands together in mocking applause.

"Excellent," he said softly. "An outstanding performance." His smile disappeared. "Just one problem, *kardia mou*. I'm on to you."

"What?"

"You heard me. I know your game. And I'm not going to play it."

"Game? Is that what you think this is? I come to you after my sister's death because you didn't have enough concern to come to me and you think—you think it's a game?"

"Perhaps I used the wrong word. It's more like a melodrama. You're the innocent little flower, I'm the cruel villain."

"I don't know what you're talking about!"

Damian started slowly toward her. He saw her stiffen. She wanted to back away or maybe even turn and run. Good, he thought coldly. She was afraid of him, and she damned well ought to be.

"Don't you want to tell me the rest? The details of our passionate encounter?"

She looked at him as if he were crazy. "What passionate encounter?"

"Come now, darling. Have you forgotten your lines? You're supposed to remind me of what we did when I was drunk." He stopped inches from her, a chill smile curling across his lips. "Well, I'm waiting. Where did it happen? Here? Athens? A party on my yacht at the Côte d'Azur? Not that it matters. The story's the same no matter where we met."

"I didn't say—"

"No. You didn't, and that's my fault. I never gave you the chance to tell your heartbreaking little tale, but why waste time when it's so trite? I was drunk. I seduced you. Now, it's—it's— How many months later, did you say?"

"Three months. You know that, just as you know the rest of what you said isn't true!"

"Did I get the facts wrong?" His eyes narrowed; his voice turned hard. "Frankly I don't give a damn. All I care about is seeing the last of you, lady. You understand?"

Ivy understood, all right.

This man her sister had worshipped, this—this Adonis whose face and body were enough to quicken the beat of a woman's heart...

This man Kay had been willing to do anything for, was looking at her and lying through his teeth.

How could Kay have loved him?

"Shall I be more direct, Miss Madison?" Damian clamped his hands on her shoulders. "Get out of here before I lose my temper."

His voice was low, his grasp painful. He was furious and, Ivy was sure, capable of violence.

That wasn't half as important as being certain she understood exactly what he was telling her.

He didn't want the child she was carrying.

She'd figured as much, when she hadn't heard from him after the accident. She'd waited and waited, caught up first in shock at losing Kay, then in growing awareness of her own desperation until, finally, she'd realized the prince's silence was a message.

Still, it wasn't enough.

He had to put his denial of his rights to his child in writing. She needed a document that said he didn't want the baby, that he'd rather believe her story was a lie than acknowledge he'd fathered a child.

Even that was no guarantee.

Damian Aristedes was powerful. He could hire all the lawyers in Manhattan and have money left over. He could not only make his own rules, he could change them when he had to.

But if she had something on paper, something that might give her a legal edge if he ever changed his mind—

"I can almost see you thinking, Miss Madison."

Ivy blinked. The prince was standing with his arms folded over his chest, narrowed eyes locked on her face.

It was disconcerting.

She was accustomed to having men look at her. It went with the territory.

When you had done hundreds of photo shoots, when your own face looked back at you from magazine covers, you expected it. It was part of the price you paid for success in the world of modeling.

Men noticed you. They looked at you.

But not like this.

The expression on Damian Aristedes's face spoke of contempt, not desire. How dare he be disdainful of her? She'd made a devil's bargain—she knew that, had known it almost from the beginning—but she'd been prepared to stand by that bargain even if it tore out her heart.

Not him.

He was the man who'd started this. Now, he was pretending he didn't know what she was talking about.

That was fine. It was perfect. It meant she'd kept her promise and now she was free to put the past behind her and concentrate on the future. On the child she'd soon have.

Her child, not his.

It was just infuriating to have him look at her as if she were a liar and a cheat.

Except, there'd been a moment, more than one, when she'd caught him watching her in a different way, his eyes glinting not with disdain but with hunger.

Hunger only she could ease.

And when that had happened, she'd felt—she'd felt—

"You're as transparent as glass, Miss Madison."

Years of letting the camera steal her face but never her thoughts kept Ivy from showing any reaction.

"How interesting. Do you read minds when you're not busy evading responsibility, Your Highness?"

"You're trying to come up with a way to capitalize on that moment of shock I showed when you told me I was your baby's father." He smiled thinly. "Trust me. You can't."

He was partly right. She was trying to come up with a way to capitalize on something, but not that.

Ivy took a steadying breath.

"I'll be happy to leave, happier still never to see you again, Prince Damian. But first—"

"Ah. But first, you want a check for... How much? A hundred thousand? Five hundred thousand? A million? Don't shake your head, Miss Madison. We both know you have a price in mind."

Another steadying breath. "Not a check."

"Cash, then. It doesn't matter."

The icy little smile slipped from his lips and she repressed a shudder. The prince would be a formidable enemy.

"I don't want money. I want a letter. A document that makes it clear you're giving up all rights to the child in my womb."

He laughed. Laughed, damn him!

"*Thee mou*, lady. Don't you know when to quit?"

"Sign it, date it and I'll be out of your life forever."

His laughter stopped with the speed of a faucet

turning off. "Enough," he said through his teeth. "Get out of my home before I do something we'll both regret."

"Just a letter," she said. "A few lines—"

He said something in what she assumed was Greek. She didn't understand the words but she didn't have to as he gripped her by the shoulders, spun her around, put a hand in the small of her back and shoved her forward.

"And if you're foolish enough to tell your ridiculous story to anyone—"

The thing to do was hire a lawyer. Except, he'd hire a dozen for every one she could afford. He had power. Money. Status. Still, there had to be a way. There had to be!

"And if you really are knocked up, if some man was stupid enough to let your face blind him to the scheming bitch you really are—"

Ivy spun around, swung her fist and caught him in the jaw. He was big and strong and hard as nails but she caught him off guard. He blinked and staggered back. It took him all of a second to recover but it was enough to send a warm rush of pleasure through her blood.

"You—you pompous ass," she hissed. She marched forward, index finger aimed at his chest, and jabbed it right into the center of his starched white shirt, her fear gone, everything forgotten but his impossible arrogance. "This isn't about you and who you are and how much money you have. It isn't about you at all! I don't want anything from you, Prince Damian. I never—"

She gasped as he caught her by the elbows and lifted her to her toes.

"You don't want anything from me, huh?" Damian's lips drew back from his teeth as he bent his head toward hers. "That's why you came here? Because you don't want anything from me?"

"I came because I thought I owed it to you but I was wrong. I don't. And I warn you, letter or no letter, if you should change your mind a month from now, a decade from now, and try and claim my baby—"

"Damn you," he roared, "there is no baby!"

"Whatever you say."

"The truth at last!"

"Truth?" Ivy laughed in his face. "You wouldn't know it if it bit you in the tail!"

"I know that I never took you to bed."

"Let go!"

"How come you didn't factor that into your little scheme?" Damian yanked her wrist, dragged it behind her back. She flinched but she'd sooner have eaten nails than let him know he was hurting her. "You made several mistakes, Miss Madison. One, I don't drink to excess. Two, I never forget a woman I've been with." His gaze swept over her with slow deliberation before returning to her face. "Believe me, lady, if I'd had you, I'd remember."

"I'm done talking about that."

"But I'm not." He drew her closer, until they were a breath apart. "Why should I be? You said we were intimate. I said we weren't. Why not settle the question?"

"It isn't worth settling. And I never said we'd been intimate."

His lips drew back from his teeth. "Ah, Ivy, Ivy, you disappoint me. Backing down already?" His smile vanished; his eyes turned cold. "Come on, *glyka mou*. Here's your chance. Convince me we slept together. Remind me of what it was like."

"Stop it. Stop it! I'm warning you, let me—"

She gasped as Damian slipped one hand lightly around her throat.

"A woman can only taunt a man for so long before he retaliates. Surely someone with your skills should have learned that by now."

"You're wrong! You know the truth, that we never—"

Damian kissed her.

Her mouth was cool and soft, and she made a little sound of terrified protest.

That was how she made it sound, anyway.

It was all part of the act. Part of a performance. Part of who she was and why she was here and…

And she tasted sweet, sweeter than the first time he'd kissed her, maybe because he knew the shape of her mouth now. The fullness of it.

The sexy silkiness.

She cried out again, jammed her hand against his chest and Damian told himself it was time to let go of her.

He'd accomplished what he wanted, met her challenge, showed her that she had no power over him…

His arousal was swift. He put one hand at the base of her spine and pressed hard enough so she had no choice but to tilt her hips against his and feel it.

God, he was on fire.

Another little sound whispered from her mouth to his and then, same as before, he felt the change in her. Her mouth softened. Warmed. The stiffness went out of her body and she leaned toward him.

He reminded himself that nothing she did was real. It was all part of her overall plan.

And it didn't matter.

He knew only that he wanted this. The taste of her.

The feel of her. He was entitled to that. Hell, he'd been accused of something he had not done.

Why not do it now?

Lift Ivy into his arms. Carry her up the stairs to his bedroom. Take everything she wanted him to believe he'd taken before, again and again and again…

"Please," she whispered, "please—"

Her voice was soft. Dazed. It made him want her even more.

Deliberately he slid his hand inside her jacket and cupped the delicate weight of one breast.

"Please, what?" he growled. "Touch you? Take you?"

His fingers swept over her breast, blood thundering in his ears when he felt the thrust of her nipple through the silk that covered it. She moaned against his mouth.

A wave of lust rolled through him, shocking him with its intensity.

She moaned again and he gathered her closer. Slid his hands under the waistband of her black jeans. Felt the coolness of her buttocks, the silk of her flesh.

Primal desire flooded his senses. He wanted her, no matter what she was. And she wanted him. Wanted him. Wanted him…

Panagia mou! Damian flung her from him and stepped back. Tears were streaming down her face. If he hadn't known better, he'd have honestly thought she was weeping.

"I can't believe Kay loved you, that she wanted to give you a child!"

"Your story's getting old. And confused. You're the one who's pregnant. Who I took to bed, remember?"

"That's not true! Why do you keep saying it? You know we didn't go to bed!"

"Right," he said, his voice cold with contempt and sarcasm. "I keep forgetting that. We didn't. We did it standing up. Or sitting in a chair. Or on a sofa—"

"There was no chair. No sofa. You know that. There was just—just your sperm. A syringe. And—and me."

"Yeah. Sure. You, my sperm, a syringe…" Damian jerked back. "What?"

"You damned well know what! And you didn't even have the—the decency to let Kay be artificially inseminated by a physician. Oh, no. You wanted to protect your precious privacy! So you—you used a—a condom to—to—" Her voice turned bitter. "I knew what you were when you didn't ask to meet me in advance. When you didn't care enough to come with Kay the day she—the day I—the day it took place."

Damian wanted to say something but he couldn't. He felt as if his head were in a vise.

Her story was fantastic. Far more interesting than the usual *He made me pregnant* tale.

And the media loved fantasy.

They'd fall on this like hyenas on a wounded antelope. By the time a different scandal knocked the story off the front pages, the damage would have been done. To his name, to Aristedes Shipping, the company he'd spent his adult life rebuilding.

"Nothing to say, Your Highness?" Ivy put her hands on her hips and eyed him with derision. "Or have you finally figured out that denial will only take you so far?"

Tossing this woman out on her backside was no longer a viable option. She was too clever for such easy dismissal.

"You're right about that," he said calmly. "Denial only goes so far and then it's time to take appropriate action." He closed the distance between them, relishing the way she stumbled back. "You will take a pregnancy test. Then, if you're really pregnant, a paternity test."

Ivy stared at him. She couldn't think of a reason he'd want her to take such tests… Unless he was telling the truth. Unless he really hadn't known about the baby.

And if he hadn't… What would happen once he did?

"I don't want to take any tests," she said quickly. "You said you didn't want the baby. That's fine. You only have to give me a document—"

"No, *glyka mou*. It is you who will provide *me* with a document that legally establishes that you and I and a syringe never met, except inside your scheming little brain."

"But—"

Damian took her arm, marched her to the elevator and pushed her inside it. Seconds later, the doors slid shut in her face.

CHAPTER FOUR

IT TROUBLED her all the way back to her apartment.

If Kay's lover had known about the baby, if he'd orchestrated it as Kay claimed, why would the details of the baby's conception have shaken him?

And he had been shaken.

He'd recovered fast but not fast enough to hide his initial shock.

And why would he want these tests? Unless, Ivy thought as she unlocked the door to her apartment, unless he'd just been getting rid of her...

But the light on her telephone was blinking. A man identifying himself as the prince's attorney had left a message on her voice mail.

She was to be at one of the city's most prestigious hospitals at eight the next morning.

Someone would meet her in the reception area.

Ivy sank into a chair. The day had finally caught up to her. She was worn-out and close to tears, wondering why she'd ever thought that seeking out Damian Aristedes was the right thing to do...

But she'd done it.

Now, she could only put one foot ahead of the other and see where this path led.

* * *

A tall, dark-haired man, his back to her, was standing in the main lobby of the hospital when she arrived there the next day.

Her heart leaped. Was it Damian?

The man turned. He was balding and he wore glasses. It wasn't the prince. Of course not. Why would she want him here? And why would he be here when he hadn't shown up with Kay for the procedure he'd demanded?

The procedure that had taken a drastic turn at the last minute.

The memory struck hard. Ivy wrapped her arms around herself. She should never have agreed to it.

Or to this.

This was another mistake.

But it was too late to run. The tall man had seen her. He came toward her, her name a question on his lips. From the look on his face, he was as uncomfortable with this whole thing as she was.

He introduced himself. He was, he said, holding out his hand, the prince's attorney, here to offer whatever assistance she might require.

"You mean," Ivy said, deliberately ignoring his outstretched hand, "you're here to make sure I don't try to phony-up the test results."

He had the good grace not to try to contradict her as he escorted her to a small office where a briskly efficient technician took over.

"Come with me, please, Miss Madison. The gentleman can wait outside."

"Oh, he's not a gentleman," Ivy said politely. "He's a lawyer."

Even the attorney laughed.

Then Ivy blanked her mind to everything but what had to be done.

The results, they said, would take up to two weeks.

She said that was fine, though two centuries would have been more to her liking.

They told her to take it easy for a couple of days and she did, even though it gave her more time to think than she wanted.

Day three, she organized the drawers and closets of her apartment. They didn't need it: she'd always been neat, something you learned quickly when you spent part of your growing-up years in foster care, but straightening things was a good way to kill time.

Day four, her agent called with a job. The cover of *La Belle* magazine. It was a plum but Ivy turned it down. She was tired all the time, her back ached and besides, she'd never much liked modeling. But she needed the money. She'd given most of what she'd saved to Kay.

Kay, who had come to her in tears.

She lived, she'd said, with Damian Aristedes. Ivy had heard of him before. You couldn't read *People* or *Vanity Fair* without seeing his name. The magazines said he was incredibly good-looking and incredibly wealthy. Kay said yes, he was both, but he was tight with a dollar and he'd refused to pay the money she still owed on her condo even though he demanded she not work.

He wanted her available to him at all times.

Ivy had given her the money. It was an enormous amount, but how could she have said no? She owed Kay so much… Money could never begin to repay that debt.

A few weeks later, Kay came to her again and

confided the rest of her story. How she'd miscarried. How Damian now demanded proof she could give him an heir before he'd marry her.

Ivy thought the man sounded like a brute but Kay adored him. She'd wept, talked about how much she wanted his baby, how much she wished she could give him such a gift.

She'd reminded Ivy of the years they'd shared as teenagers, of memories Ivy was still doing her best to forget.

"Do you remember how desperate you were then?" Kay had said through her tears. "That's how desperate I am now! Please, please, you have to help me."

In the end, Ivy had agreed to something she'd convinced herself was good even if it might prove emotionally difficult, but she'd never expected it to go as far as it had. To turn into something she'd regretted almost immediately, something she wept over night after night—

Something she might well end up fighting in court, and how would she pay those legal fees?

Ivy picked up the phone, called her agent and told him she'd do the *La Belle* cover after all.

It was excellent money and it was a head shot; nobody would see that she was pregnant.

Still, head shot or not, the photographer insisted she be styled right down to her toes. She spent the day in heavy makeup and endless outfits matched by spectacular sky-high Manolos on her feet.

When she finally reached her Chelsea brownstone, it was after five. She was exhausted and headachy, her face felt like a mask under all the expensive makeup she hadn't taken time to remove and her feet…

Her feet were two blobs of pain.

She was still wearing the last pair of Manolos from the final set of photos. Actually she was swollen into them.

"Poor darling," the stylist cooed. "Keep them as a gift."

So she'd limped into a taxi, limped out of it. Now, if she could just get up the three flights of steps to her apartment…

Three flights of steps. They never even made her breathe hard. Now, they loomed ahead like Mount McKinley.

Ivy took a deep breath and started climbing.

She was shaking with fatigue when she finally reached her landing, and wincing at the pain in her feet. She waited a minute, then took out her key and fumbled it into the lock.

Soon. Oh, yes, soon. Off with the shoes. Into the shower, then into a loose T-shirt and an even looser pair of fleece sweatpants. After that, she'd put together a peanut butter and honey sandwich on the kind of soft, yummy white bread that the health gurus hated…

Ivy shut the door behind her, automatically slid home the chain lock, turned around…

And screamed.

A man—dark hair, broad shoulders, long legs, leather jacket and pale blue jeans—was seated in a chair in her living room.

"Easy," he said, rising quickly to his feet, but it was too late. The floor had already rushed up to meet her.

"Thee mou," a voice said gruffly.

Strong arms closed around her.

After that, there was only darkness.

* * *

Damian had never moved faster in his life.

A damned good thing he had, he thought grimly, though the woman he held in his arms was as limp as the proverbial dishrag.

A man might joke about wanting a woman to fall at his feet, but this was surely not the way it should happen.

Especially if the woman was pregnant.

He cursed ripely in his native tongue and shoved that thought aside. He had come here to deal with that fact and he would. Right now, what mattered was that Ivy had passed out cold.

She felt warm and soft in his arms, but her face was frighteningly pale. Her breathing seemed shallow. What was he supposed to do now? Call 9-1-1? Wait until she stirred? Did he search her apartment for spirits of ammonia?

Ivy solved the problem by raising her lashes. She looked at him and he saw confusion in her deep green eyes.

"Damian?"

It was the first time she'd called him that.

"Damian, what—what happened?"

"You fainted, *glyka mou*. My fault. I apologize."

She closed her eyes, then opened them again. This time, the confusion was gone.

Anger had taken its place.

"I remember now. I unlocked the door and—"

"You saw me."

"How did you get in here? I never leave the door unlocked!"

"The super let me in." His mouth twisted. "A story

about being your long-lost brother and a hundred-dollar bill melted his heart."

"You had no right—"

"Unfortunately you don't have a back entrance and a flight of service steps," he said dryly.

"It's hardly the same thing."

"It's exactly the same thing."

Ivy stiffened in his arms. "Please put me down."

"Would you prefer the bedroom or the sofa?"

"I would prefer my feet on the floor."

He almost laughed. She was still pale but there was no mistaking the indignation in her voice.

"You will lie down while I phone for a doctor."

Ivy shook her head. "I don't need a doctor. I fainted, that's all."

She was right. He decided not to argue. They'd have enough to argue over in a little while.

"You're a stubborn woman, Miss Madison."

"Not half as stubborn as you, Your Highness."

Damian carried her to a small, brocade-covered sofa and sat her on it.

"Amazing, how you manage to make 'Your Highness' sound like a four-letter word. No. Do not even try to stand up. I'm going to get a cold compress."

"I told you—"

"And I'm telling you, sit there and behave yourself."

He strode off, found a towel in the kitchen, filled it with ice and returned to the living room, surprised to find she'd heeded his warning.

It was, he thought, a bad sign.

Almost as bad as the feverish color that was replacing the pallor in her skin. He wanted to take her in his arms, hold her close, tell her he was sorry he'd frightened her…

Hell.

"Here," he said brusquely, thrusting the ice-filled towel into her hands.

"I don't need that," she snapped, but she took the towel anyway and pressed it to her wrists.

He took the time to take a long look at her.

She looked worn out. Dark shadows were visible under her eyes despite a layer of heavy makeup. She hadn't worn makeup the other day. Why would she, when her natural beauty was so breathtaking?

His gaze swept over her.

She had on a loose-fitting, heavy sweater. A matching skirt. And, *Thee mou,* what was she doing, wearing those shoes? They were the kind that would normally make his blood pressure rise but that wasn't going to happen when he could see the straps denting her flesh.

Damian looked up. "Your feet are swollen."

"How clever of you to notice."

"Are you so vain you'd wear shoes that hurt?"

"I am not vain—what are you doing?"

"Taking off these ridiculous shoes."

"Stop it!" Ivy tried slapping his hands away as he lifted one of her feet to his lap. "I said—"

"I heard you."

His fingers moved swiftly, undoing straps and tiny jeweled buckles. The shoe fell off. Gently he lowered her leg, then removed the second shoe. When he'd finished, Ivy planted both her bare feet on the floor.

It was all she could do to keep from groaning with relief.

"Better?"

She didn't answer. *Thee mou,* he had never known such an intractable female.

Damian muttered something under his breath and lifted her feet to his lap again.

"Of course they're better," he said, answering his own question. His tone was brusque but his hands were gentle as he massaged her ankles, her toes, her insteps. "Why a woman would put herself through such torture—"

"I just came from a cover shoot. The stylist gave me the shoes as a gift. They do that kind of thing sometimes," she said, wondering why on earth she was explaining herself to this arrogant man.

"And you were so thrilled you decided to wear them home even though they were killing you."

Ivy's eyes narrowed. "Yes," she said coldly, "that's right." She tugged her feet from his hands and sat up. "Now that you've told me what you think of my decisions, try telling me something that matters, like what you're doing here."

A muscle knotted in his jaw. Then he took an envelope from his pocket and tossed it on the coffee table.

Ivy caught her breath.

"Are those the test results?"

He nodded.

"They were supposed to send them to me."

"And to me."

"Well, that's wrong. That's an invasion of privacy. The results of *my* test are *my* business—"

Ivy knew she was babbling. She stopped, reached for the envelope but she couldn't bring herself to touch it. They'd tested for pregnancy. For paternity. For the first time, she realized they could also have tested for maternity…

Her hands began to shake. She sat back.

"Tell me," she said softly.

"You already know." His voice was without intonation, though she sensed a restrained violence in his words. "I am the father of the child in your womb. The child that would have been Kay's."

Ivy swallowed hard. "And the sex?" she whispered.

"It is a boy."

A little sound broke from her throat and she put her hand over her mouth. It was, Damian thought coldly, one hell of an act.

"I tried to tell you I was pregnant. That you were the father. You wouldn't listen."

"I am listening now." Damian sat back and folded his arms. "Tell me again, from the beginning. I want to hear everything."

She did, from the moment Kay proposed the idea until the moment she'd confronted him in his apartment, though there were some parts—all right, one part—she left out.

She didn't dare tell him that. Not yet.

Maybe not ever.

But she went through all the facts, pausing to answer his questions, biting her lip each time he shook his head in disbelief because, in her heart, she still shared that disbelief.

What Kay had asked of her, what she'd agreed to do, was insane.

"Why?" he said, when she'd finished the tale. "Why would Kay ask you to be a— What did you call it?"

"A gestational surrogate. Her egg. Your—your sperm." She knew she was blushing, and wasn't that ridiculous? The procedure Kay had planned, even the one they'd actually ended up doing, was about as intimate as a flu shot. "And I told you why. You wanted a child. She knew she couldn't carry one."

Damian shot to his feet. "Lies! I never said anything about a child. And she didn't know if she could carry one or not."

"You asked me to tell you everything. That's what I'm doing."

She gasped as he hauled her to her feet.

"The hell you are," he snarled. "What did she pay you for your role in this?"

"Pay me?" Ivy laughed. "Not a penny. You kept Kay on a tight allowance."

"Another lie!"

"Even if you hadn't, I'd never have done this for money."

"No," he said grimly. "You did it out of love."

"I know you can't understand something like that but—"

"I understand, all right. You hatched out a plot between you. You'd have a baby Kay didn't want to have, she'd use it to force me into marriage. And when she divorced me, the two of you would split whatever huge settlement a shyster lawyer could bleed out of me."

Ivy jerked free of his hands. "Do you have any idea how much I earn in a day? How much I'll lose by not modeling for the next five or six months? Hell, for the next couple of years?"

"Is that why you took an assignment today?" he said, sneering. "Because you have so much money you don't need any more?"

"That's none of your business!"

"You're wrong," he said coldly. "From now on, everything about you is my business."

"No, it isn't."

"What did I just say? Starting now, everything about you is also about me."

"The hell it is!"

Ivy glared at him. Damian glared back. Her chin was raised. Her eyes were cold. Her hands were knotted on her hips.

She looked like one of the Furies, ready and determined to take on the world.

He wanted to cover the distance between them, grab her and shake her. Or grab her, haul her into his arms and kiss her until she trembled.

He hated the effect she had on him, hated himself for bending to it… And it was time to put all that aside.

He knew what he had to do.

It was time she knew it, too.

"We're getting sidetracked," he said.

"I agree, Your Highness."

That drove him crazy, too. The way she said "Your Highness." He hadn't been joking when he'd told her she made it sound like a four-letter word.

"Under the circumstances," he said brusquely, "I think you should call me Damian."

She got his meaning; he knew because he saw her cheeks flame. Good, he thought grimly. He wanted her a little uncertain. Why should he be the only one who was balancing on a tightrope?

"This is a pointless conversation. Why should it matter what I call you? Once we determine what happens after my—after the baby's born, we don't have to see each other again."

"Is that what you would you like to happen?"

Was he really asking? Ivy could hardly believe it but she was ready with an answer. This was all she'd thought about since the day she'd gone to his apartment.

"I'd like a simple solution," she said carefully, "one that would please us both."

"And that is?"

She could hear her heart pounding. Could he hear it, too?

"You—you've fathered a baby you say you didn't want."

"More correctly, I fathered a baby I didn't know about."

If that was true—and she had to believe it was—it worried her. The way he'd just stated the situation worried her, too. Fathering a baby he didn't want wasn't the same as fathering a baby he hadn't known about.

She wanted to call him on it but that wouldn't help her case, and that was the last thing she wanted to do.

"A baby you didn't know about," she said, trying to sound as if she really believed it. "A baby my sister wanted."

"But?" He smiled thinly. "I could hear the word, even if it was unspoken."

She drew a breath, then let it out. "But, everything's changed. Kay is gone and I—I want this baby. I didn't know I'd feel this way. That I'd love the baby without ever seeing it. That I wouldn't want to give it away or—"

"Very nice," he said coldly. "But please, spare me the performance. How much?"

She looked puzzled. "I just told you. I want the baby with all my heart."

Damian came toward her, shaking his head and

smiling. "You have it wrong. I'm not asking about your heart, I'm asking about your wallet. How much must I pay you to give up this child you carry?"

"This has nothing to do with money."

"You are Kay's sister. Everything has to do with money." His mouth twisted. "How much?"

"I want my baby, Damian! You don't want it. You said so."

"You don't listen, *glyka mou*. I said, I didn't know about the child." Slowly he reached out and slid his hand beneath Ivy's sweater. She grabbed his wrist and tried to move it but it was like trying to move an oak.

His fingers spread over her belly.

"That's my son," he said softly. "In your womb. He carries my genes. My blood."

"And mine," she said quickly.

"You mean, Kay's."

She flushed. "Yes. Of course that's what I mean."

"A baby you meant to give up."

The words hurt her heart.

"Yes," she whispered, so softly he could hardly hear her. "I thought I could. But—but just as you said, this baby is in my womb—"

Damian caught her face in his hands.

"My seed," he said. "Your womb. In other words, our child." His gaze, like a caress, fell to her lips. "Via a syringe, Ivy. Not you in my arms, in my bed, the way it should have been."

"But it wasn't." Was that high, breathless voice really hers? "Besides, that has nothing to do with the facts."

She was right.

But he'd given up trying to be logical. Nothing about

this was logical, he thought, and he bent to her and kissed her.

The kiss was long. Deep. And when she made a soft, sweet sound that could only have been a sigh of desire, Damian took the kiss deeper still. His tongue slipped into her mouth; he tasted her sweetness, God, her innocence...

Except, she wasn't innocent.

She'd entered into an unholy bargain with her sister and he didn't for a minute believe she'd done it as some great humanitarian gesture...

And then he stopped thinking, gathered her tightly in his arms and kissed her again and again until she was gripping his shoulders, until she was parting her lips to his, until she rose to him, pressed against him, sighed into his mouth.

She swayed when he let go of her. Her eyes flew open; she looked as shaken as he felt.

He hated her for it.

For the act, the drama...the effect it had on him.

"So," he said, his tone calm despite the pounding surge of his blood, "we have a dilemma. How do I claim a child that's mine when it's still in your womb?"

"You don't. I just told you, I want—"

"Frankly I don't give a damn what you want. Neither will a judge. You entered into a devil's bargain with your sister. Now you'll pay the price."

Her green eyes went black with fear. At least, it looked like fear. He knew it was greed.

"No court is going to take a child from its mother."

"You're not his mother, *glyka mou*. But I am its father."

"Still—"

"There is no 'still,' Ivy. No if, no but, no maybe. I've spoken with my attorney."

"Your attorney isn't God."

Damian laughed. "Try telling him that." His laughter faded. "Do you have any idea how much I pay him each year?"

"No, and I don't give a damn! Your money doesn't impress me."

"I pay him a million dollars. And that's only a retainer." He reached for her. She stepped back but he caught her with insolent ease and pulled her into his arms again. "He's worth every penny. And I promise, he will take my son from you."

"No." Tears rose in Ivy's eyes. "You can't do this. You wouldn't do this!"

"But I'm not heartless," Damian said softly. "I'm even willing to believe there's some truth to what you say about not wanting to give up my child." He bent his head to hers; she tried to twist her face away but he slid his hands into her hair and held her fast. "So I've decided to make you an offer." He smiled. "An offer, as they say, you cannot refuse."

The world, the room, everything seemed to stop.

"What?" Ivy whispered.

Damian took her mouth with his. Kissed her as she struggled. As she wept. As she tried to break free until, at last, she went still in his arms and let the kiss happen.

It wasn't what he wanted, damn it.

He wanted her to kiss him back, as she had before. To melt against him, to moan, to show him that she wanted him, wanted him...

Even if it was a lie.

He drew back. She stood motionless.

"I return to Greece tomorrow."

"You can return to Hades for all I care. I want to know what you're offering me."

What he'd come up with was surprisingly simple. He'd worked it out late last night, on the impossible chance her story about her pregnancy turned out to be true.

This morning, after the test results had proved that it was, he'd run the idea past his attorney who'd said yes, okay, with just a couple of touch-ups, it would work.

Ivy would put herself into the hands of a physician of his choosing. She would stop working—he would support her through the pregnancy. He'd move her into a place nearer his condo. And when she gave birth, he would give her a one time payment of ten million dollars and she would give him his son.

He'd even permit her to visit the child four times a year, if she was really as emotionally committed to him as she made it seem.

More than generous, his attorney had agreed.

"Damn you," Ivy demanded, "what offer?"

Damian cleared his throat. "Ten million dollars on the birth of my child."

She laughed. Damn her, she laughed!

"Until then, I will move you to a place of my choosing. And, of course, I will support you."

Another peal of laughter burst from her throat. He could feel every muscle in his body tensing.

"You find this amusing?"

"I find it amazing! Do you really think you can buy my baby? That you can take over my life?"

"The child is not yours. You seem to keep forgetting

that. As for your so-called life…" His eyes darkened. "Your sister had a life, too, one that was inappropriate."

"And you are a candidate for sainthood?"

Damian could feel his control slipping. Who was she, this woman who thought she could defy him? Who had entered into a conspiracy that would change his life?

"I know who I am," he said coldly. "More to the point, I know who you are." His eyes flickered over her in dismissal. "You are a woman who agreed to bear a child for money."

"I'm tired of defending myself, tired of explaining, tired of being bullied." Ivy's voice trembled with emotion. "I don't want your money or your support, and I'm certainly not moving to an apartment where you can keep me prisoner!"

She kept talking. He stopped listening. All he could see was her face, tearstained and determined.

Did she think he was a complete fool? That this show of rebelliousness would convince him to up the ante?

"I am not some—some meek little lamb," she said, "eager to do your bidding." She folded her arms and glared at him. "Do you understand, Your Highness? My answer to your offer is no!"

She gasped as he captured her face in his hands.

"It wasn't an offer," he growled. "It is what you will do—but I'm changing the terms. Forget the apartment near mine. I am taking you to Greece with me."

She stared at him as if he'd lost his mind. He hadn't. He'd simply begun to see things more clearly.

He was in New York once a month at best. What would she be doing while he was away? He had the right to know.

She slung an obscenity at him that almost made him laugh, coming as it did from that perfect mouth.

"I will not go anywhere with you. There are laws—"

"What laws?" His mouth thinned. "I am Prince Damian Aristedes. Do you think your laws have any meaning to me?"

Ivy couldn't speak. There was no word to describe what she felt for this man. Hatred didn't even come close—but he was a prince. He could trace his lineage back through the centuries. She was nobody. She could trace her lineage back to a foster home where—where—

No. She wasn't going there.

Damian's hands tightened. He raised her face until their eyes met.

"Do you understand what I've told you? Or are you going to be foolish enough to try to fight me?"

"I despise you!"

"Ah, *glyka mou,* you're breaking my heart."

"You're a monster. I can't stand having you touch me."

"A decision, Ivy. And quickly."

Tears spilled down her face. "You know my decision! You haven't left me a choice."

Damian felt a swell of triumph but it was poisoned by the hatred in Ivy's eyes. With a growl of rage, he captured her mouth, kissing her without mercy, without tenderness, nipping her bottom lip when she refused the thrust of his tongue.

"A reminder," he said coldly. "Until my son is born, you belong to me."

Even in his anger, he knew a good line when he heard it.

He turned around and walked out.

CHAPTER FIVE

DAMIAN went down the stairs with fury clouding his eyes, went out the door to the street the same way.

His driver had brought him to Ivy's apartment. The Mercedes was at the curb and Damian started toward it. Charles must have been watching for him; he sprang from behind the wheel, rushed around to the rear door and swung it open.

Charles had only been with him a couple of months but surely Damian had told him he was capable of opening a car door himself a hundred times.

A thousand times, he thought, as his temper super-heated.

Then he saw the way Charles was looking at him.

"My apologies, Your Highness. I keep forgetting. It's just that you are the first employer I've had who doesn't want me getting out to open or close the door. I promise, it won't—"

"No, that's all right," Damian said. "Don't worry about it." He paused beside the car. He had a meeting later in the day. There was just time for him to go to his office and do some work.

But work wasn't what he needed right now. What he needed was a drink.

"I won't be needing the car," he said briskly, and slapped the top of the Mercedes.

"Very well, sir. I'll wait until you—"

"I won't need the car at all." He forced a smile. After all, none of this was his driver's fault. "Take it back to the garage and call it a day."

Charles looked surprised but he was too well-trained to ask questions. A good thing, Damian thought as he walked away, because he sure as hell didn't have any answers. Not logical ones, anyway.

Logic had nothing to do with the mess he was in.

At the corner, he took out his cell phone, called his assistant and told her to cancel his appointment. Then he called Lucas.

"Are you busy?"

He tried to make the question sound casual but his old friend's response told him he hadn't succeeded.

"What's wrong?" Lucas said sharply.

"Nothing. Why should anything be..." Damian cleared his throat. "I don't want to discuss it over the phone, but if you're busy—"

"I am not busy," Lucas said.

A lie, Damian was certain, but one he readily accepted.

Forty minutes later, the two men were pounding along the running track at the Eastside Club. At this hour of the day, they pretty much had the place to themselves.

Despite the privacy, they hadn't exchanged more than a dozen words. Damian knew Lucas was giving him the chance to start the conversation but he'd been content just to work up a sweat, first with the weights, then on the track.

There was nothing like a hard workout for getting rid of anger.

He'd learned that in the days when he'd been rebuilding Aristedes Shipping. There'd been times back then he'd deliberately gone from a meeting with the money men who held his destiny in their greedy hands to unloading cargo from a barge on the Aristedes docks.

Right now, he thought grimly, right now, he could use a ton of cargo.

"Damian."

More than that. Two tons of—

"Damian! Man, what're we doing? Working out, or trying for heart attacks?"

Damian blinked, slowed, looked around and saw Lucas standing in the middle of the track, head bent, hands on his thighs, dripping with sweat and panting.

And, *Thee mou*, so was he. How many miles had they run? How fast? Neither of them got like this doing their usual six-minute mile.

He stepped off the track, grabbed a couple of towels from a cart and tossed one to Lucas.

"Sorry, man."

"You should be," Lucas said, rubbing his face with the towel. He grinned. "Actually I didn't think an old man like you could move that fast."

Damian grinned back at him. "I'm two months older than you are, Reyes."

"Every day counts when you're pushing thirty-two."

Damian smiled. He draped the towel around his shoulders and he and Lucas strolled toward the locker room.

"Thank you," he said, after a minute.

Lucas shot his friend a look, thought about pretending he didn't know what he meant and decided honesty was the best policy.

"*Para nada,*" he said softly. "The way you sounded,

I'd have canceled a meeting with the president." He pushed open the locker room door, then followed Damian inside. "You want to tell me what's going on?"

Damian hesitated. "Let's shower, change and stop for a drink."

"Here?"

He laughed at the horror in Lucas's voice. The Eastside Club had a bar. A juice bar.

"No. Not here. I'm old but not that old."

Lucas grinned. "I'm relieved to hear it. How about that place a couple of blocks over? The one with the mahogany booths?"

"Sounds good."

It was good.

The bar was dark, the way bars should be. The booths were deep and comfortable. The bartender was efficient and the Gray Goose on the rocks both men ordered was crisp and cold.

They were mostly quiet at first, Lucas talking about some land he was thinking of adding to his enormous ranch in Spain, Damian listening, nodding every now and then, saying "yes" and "really" when it seemed appropriate.

Then they fell silent.

Lucas finally cleared his throat. "So," he said quietly, "you okay?"

"I'm fine."

"Because, you know, you didn't sound—"

"Kay's sister turned up."

Lucas lifted his eyebrows. "I didn't know she had a—"

"Neither did I."

"Well. Her sister, huh? What's she want?"

"I think they were actually stepsisters. That's what Ivy—"

"The sister."

"Yes. That's what she said."

"Same mother?"

"Same father. I think. Same last name, anyway. Maybe he adopted one of them…" Damian huffed out a breath. "It doesn't matter."

"What does?"

"The rest of what this woman—Ivy—told me."

Damian lifted his glass and took a long swallow of vodka. Lucas waited a while before he spoke again.

"You want to explain what that means?"

"The rest?" Damian shrugged. He took another mouthful of vodka. Took a handful of cashews from the dish on the table. Looked around the room, then at Lucas. "The rest is that she's pregnant with my child."

If Lucas's jaw dropped any further, Damian figured it would have hit the table.

"Excuse me?"

"Yeah." Damian gave a choked laugh. "Impossible, right?"

Lucas snorted. "How about, insane?"

"I told her that. And—"

"And?"

"And, you're right. *I'm* right. It's impossible. Insane. There's just one problem." Damian took a deep breath and expelled it as his eyes met Lucas's. "She's telling the truth."

Damian explained everything.

Then, at Lucas's request, he explained it all over

again, starting with Ivy's unexpected visit to his apartment and finishing with his impossible dilemma.

Lucas listened, made an occasional comment in Spanish. Damian didn't always understand the words but he didn't have to.

The other man's reaction was just what his had been.

Finally Damian fell silent. Lucas started to speak, took a drink of vodka instead, then cleared his throat.

"I don't understand. Your mistress convinced Ivy to have a baby for her but didn't tell you about it. What was she going to do when the child was born? Bundle him up, carry him through the door and say, 'Damian, this is our son'?"

Damian nodded. "I don't get it, either, but Kay wasn't big on logic. For all I know, she never got that far in laying out her plan."

"And Ivy…" Lucas's eyes narrowed. "What sort of woman is she?"

A beautiful woman, Damian thought, tall and lithe as a tigress with eyes as green as new spring grass, hair shot with gold…

"She's attractive."

"I didn't mean that. What I'm asking is, what kind of woman would agree to be part of a scheme like that?"

Damian lifted his glass to his lips. "Another excellent question."

"A model, you say. So she must be good-looking."

"You could say that."

"A model's body is her bread and butter. Why would she put herself through a pregnancy?"

"I don't—"

"I do. For money, Damian. You're worth a fortune. She wants to tap into that."

"I offered her ten million dollars to have the baby and give up all rights to it. She said no."

"Ten million," Lucas said impatiently. "That's a fraction of what you're worth and I'd bet you anything the lady researched your worth to the nearest penny." He lifted his glass, found it empty and signaled for another round. "She's good-looking, and she's smart."

"So?"

"So, my friend, if she's smart, good-looking and devious as the devil, give some thought to the entire idea having been hers in the first place."

"No. It was Kay."

"Think about it, Damian. She knew your lover could not carry a child and so she planted this idea in your lover's head—"

"Don't keep calling Kay my lover," Damian said, more sharply than he'd intended. "I mean, technically, she was. But the fact is, we had an affair. A brief one. I was going to end it but she lied and said she was—"

"Yes. I know." Lucas paused until the barman had delivered their fresh drinks. Then he leaned over the table. "Ivy observed it all. She watched you do the right thing when her sister pretended to be pregnant." He sat back, looking grimly certain of his next words. "Absolutely, the more I think about it, the more certain I am that this plan was her idea."

"Ivy's?"

"*Si.* Who else am I talking about? She saw the way to get her hands on a lot of money. She would carry a child. You would not know about it but once it was born, you would once again do the right thing. You would accept it into your life, and you would pay her anything she asked. Billions, not a paltry few million, and she and Kay would be on easy street."

Damian ran the tip of his finger along the chill edge of the glass.

"It sounds," he said, "like it could almost work. The perfect plan." He looked up, his eyes as cold as his voice. "I didn't buy into Ivy's crap about doing this out of love for her sister but I couldn't come up with anything better, especially after she turned down the ten million."

"And so now, what will you do? What did you tell this woman?"

Damian shrugged. "What could I tell her?"

"That you would support her until the child is born. That you would support the child. Pay for his care. Send him to the best boarding schools…" Lucas frowned. "Why are you shaking your head?"

"Is that what you would do with a child of your own blood? Pay to keep him out of your life?"

"Yes, of course…" Lucas sighed and rubbed his hands over his face. "No," he said softly. "I would not. His arrival in the world would be a gift, no matter how it happened."

"Exactly." Damian reached for the fresh drink, changed his mind and signaled for their check. "So," he said, carefully avoiding eye contact, "I did the only thing I could. I told her I'd take her to Greece."

Lucas almost leaped across the table. "You told her what?"

"I can't stay in New York the next six months, Lucas. You know that."

"Yes, but—"

"I need to keep an eye on her. I don't know what

she's like. How she's treating this pregnancy. If she's anything like her sister…"

The barman handed him the leather folder that held the check; Damian opened it, took a quick look and handed the man a bill, indicated he should keep the change and began rising to his feet.

Lucas grabbed his arm.

"Wait a minute! I don't think you've thought this through."

"Believe me, I have."

"Damian. Listen. You take her to Greece, she's in your life. Right in the middle of your life, man! And you don't want that."

"You're right, I don't. But what choice do I have? She needs watching."

"You're playing into her hands."

"No way! She fought me, tooth and nail. I'm forcing her to do something she absolutely doesn't want to do."

"Aristedes, you're not thinking straight. Of course she wants to do it! A model who sold her body for another woman's use? Why would she do such a thing, huh?" Lucas's eyes narrowed. "I'll tell you why. For money. And now, with her sister out of the picture, the stakes are even higher."

Damian wanted to argue but how could he when he held those same convictions? And since that was the case, why did he feel his muscles knotting at Lucas's cold words?

"She's playing you like a Stradivarius, Damian."

"Perhaps," Damian said carefully. "But that doesn't change the facts. She's carrying my—"

"She can carry him here as well as in Greece. You want her watched? Hire a private investigator but for

God's sake, don't play into her hands. She's no good, Damian. The woman is an avaricious, scheming bitch."

"Don't call her that," Damian snapped.

Lucas looked at him as if he'd lost his mind. Hell, maybe he had. Lucas had just given a perfect description of Ivy…

Except for those brief moments she'd softened in his arms, let his mouth taste the sweetness of hers. Those moments when she'd responded to him…

Pretended to respond, he thought coldly, and forced a laugh.

"I'm joking," he said lightly. "You know that American expression? Apple pie, the flag, motherhood? You're supposed to show respect for all three."

Lucas didn't look convinced. "Just as long as it's a joke," he finally said.

Damian nodded. "It was. Thank you for worrying about me but trust me, Lucas. I know what I'm doing."

I know what I'm doing.

The words haunted him the rest of the day. At midnight, after tossing and turning, Damian rose from his bed, made a pot of coffee and took a cup out onto the terrace that wrapped around his apartment.

Did he really know what he was doing? He'd had mistresses and lovers but he'd never taken a woman to live with him.

Not that he proposed to do that with Ivy.

Moving her into one of the suites in his palace was hardly taking her to live with him. Still, was it necessary? He could hire someone to watch her, as Lucas suggested. He could hire a companion to live with her.

He almost laughed.

He could imagine Ivy's reaction to that. She'd confront the private detective, order the companion out the door. She had the beauty of Diana and the courage of Athena. It was one hell of a combination.

Wind tousled his hair. Damian shivered. The night was cold and he was wearing only a pair of black sweat-pants. It was time to go inside. Or put on a sweatshirt.

Not just yet, though.

He loved New York, especially at night.

People said the city never slept but at this hour, especially on a weekday night, Central Park West grew quiet. Only a few vehicles moved along the street far below.

Was Lucas right? Had he handled this all wrong?

He could warn Ivy that any tendency she had to behave like her sister would result in severe penalties. A cut in allowance, for a start.

As for the child... Plenty of kids grew up without their fathers. He certainly had. Hell, he'd grown up without either parent, when you thought about it. His mother had been too busy jet-setting to one party after another to pay attention to him; his father had done exactly what *his* father had done, ignored him until he was old enough to send to boarding school.

He had survived, hadn't he?

Damian sipped at his coffee, gone cold and bitter.

As cold and bitter as Ivy Madison's heart?

It was a definite possibility. She might well have plotted and schemed, as Lucas insisted. For all he knew, she was out celebrating, knowing she was on her way to collecting the big prize, that he had demanded she go to Greece with him.

Out celebrating with whom?

Not that he gave a damn. It was just that the mother of his unborn child should not be out drinking or dancing or being with a man.

With a man. A faceless stranger, holding her. Kissing her. Taking her into his bed…

The cup fell from Damian's hand and shattered on the flagstone. He cursed, bent down, started scooping up the pieces…

"Son of a bitch," he snarled, and he opened the French doors and marched to his bedroom.

He dressed quickly. Jeans, a cashmere sweater, mocs and a leather bomber jacket. Then he snatched his keys from the dresser and took the elevator to the basement garage where he kept the big Mercedes as well as a black Porsche Carrera. He'd bought the car because he loved it, even though he rarely had the chance to use it.

The Carrera was a finely honed mass of energy and power.

Right now, so was he.

He'd felt that way since he first laid eyes on Ivy Madison. Who in hell was she to come out of nowhere and turn his existence upside down?

The streets were all but deserted. He made the fifteen-minute drive in half that time, pulled into a space marked No Parking on the corner of her block. The front door to her brownstone was not locked. Even if it had been, that wouldn't have stopped him.

Not tonight.

He took the three flights of steps in seconds, rang her doorbell, banged his fist on the door.

"Ivy!" He pounded the door again, called her name even louder. "Damn you, let me in!"

The door opened the inch the antitheft chain allowed.

Damian saw a sliver of dimly lighted room, a darkly lashed eye, a swath of gold-streaked hair.

"Are you crazy?" she snarled. "You'll wake the entire building!"

"Open the damned door!"

The door closed, locks and chain rattled and then the door swung open. Damian stepped inside and slammed it behind him. Ivy stared at him, hair disheveled, silk robe untied, feet bare.

She looked frightened, sleep-tossed and sexy.

The combination sent his already-racing heart into higher gear.

"Do you know what time it is?"

"The real question," he said roughly, "is, do you?"

He heard the flat challenge in his voice, saw her awareness of it reflected in the sudden catch of her breath.

"Have you been drinking?"

"Not enough."

He took a step forward. She took one back. "Your Highness…"

"I think it's time we stopped being so formal." Another step. His, followed by hers. "My name is Damian."

"Your Highness. Damian." The tip of her tongue swept across her bottom lip. He felt his entire body clench at the sight. "Damian, it's very late. Why don't we—why don't we talk tomorrow?"

One more step. Like that. And then her shoulders hit the wall.

"I'm done talking," he said, reaching for her. "And so are you."

"No! Get out. Damian! Get—"

"Isn't it amazing," he said softly, his eyes hot and locked to hers, "that I've seen a piece of paper that says you're pregnant with my child, I've had my hand on your belly." He caught a fistful of her robe, tugged her closer. "But I've never seen you."

"Of course you—"

"You," he said thickly. "Your body. How your breasts look, how your belly looks as your body readies itself for my son."

"Damian! I swear, I'll scream—"

Slowly he drew the robe open. Her eyes widened. Her lips parted. But she didn't scream. No. Oh, no. She didn't scream as he dropped his gaze and looked down at her.

She was wearing a cream-silk nightgown. Thin straps. Silk cups. Shirring over her midriff, then a long, slender fall of silk that ended just above her toes.

Damian's gaze lifted. His eyes swept her face. Her lips were still parted, her eyes still wide...

"Don't," she whispered.

But he did.

Slowly he hooked his fingers under the thin silk straps, Drew them down her arms.

Bared her breasts. Her beautiful breasts. Small. Round. Tipped with pale pink nipples that were already beading. Praxiteles, who had sculpted Aphrodite's beauty in marble, would have wept.

"Damian..."

"Shh," he whispered and cupped her breasts. Thumbed the delicate nipples. Ivy swayed unsteadily as he bent his head and touched his mouth to her nipples. Licked them. Sucked them. Felt his erection strain against his jeans.

"Damian," she said, the word a sigh. A moan.

A plea.

He lifted his head. Her lashes had drooped against her cheeks. Her breasts rose and fell with her quickened breath.

Her eyes opened, locked on his face as he pulled the gown down, down, down her torso. Her hips. Her legs. Those long, long legs.

The gown was a chrysalis at her feet.

And she—she was more than beautiful. She was Aphrodite rising from the sea. She was every dream a man could have, and more.

And yes, her body was readying for his child.

He could see the delicate swell of her belly. The exquisite rounding. The burgeoning fullness.

Slowly he cupped her belly.

Felt the smoothness of her skin. The heat of it. The perfect arc of it beneath his palms.

He stroked one hand lower. Lower still. Watched her face, heard her moan as he slipped it between her thighs and God, God, she was hot, wet, sweetly swollen with need...

"Don't," she sighed, but her hands were on his chest. On his shoulders. She was on her toes, lifting herself to him, her mouth a breath from his.

She wanted this. Wanted him.

It was all he could do to keep from taking her down to the floor, unzipping his jeans, parting her thighs and burying himself deep inside her warmth...

Except, Lucas was right. It was all an act.

Damian let go of her. Picked up her robe, wrapped it around her shoulders. Trembling, panting, she clutched it to her.

"Do you remember what I told you this afternoon?"

The tip of her tongue slid along the seam of her mouth.

"You said—you said you were taking me to Greece."

He nodded, reminded himself of Lucas's advice and stepped back. "I've changed my mind."

"You mean, you'll let me stay here?" Her breath caught. If he hadn't known better, he'd have thought it was with relief.

Of course, that was what he meant. Certainly it was what he meant…

The hell it was, he thought, and pulled her into his arms.

"I mean," he said roughly, "that I'd be a fool to pay for your upkeep without getting anything in return."

"I don't understand."

"You will share my bed. You will give birth to my son. And if, in the intervening months, you have proven yourself sufficiently accomplished as my mistress, I will marry you, give you my name, my title…and permit you to be a mother to this child you claim to want for your own." He drew her closer. "If you haven't pleased me, I will keep my son, send you back to New York and you can fight me in the courts."

Time seemed to stand still. Then Ivy looked unflinchingly into his eyes.

"I hate you," she said, "hate you, hate you—"

Damian kissed her again and again mercilessly, fiercely, until, finally, she gave a little sob and melted against him.

Was that, too, part of the act?

It didn't matter.

"Hate me all you like, *glyka mou*. From this moment on, I own you."

CHAPTER SIX

A WOMAN identifying herself as Damian's personal assistant phoned at six and offered no apology for calling at such an early hour.

"Do you have a passport, Miss Madison?"

Ivy was tempted to say she didn't but what was the point? For all she knew, traveling with royalty meant doing away with passports.

"Yes. I have."

"In that case, please be ready to leave for Greece at eight-thirty. Promptly at eight-thirty," the P.A. said emphatically. "His Highness does not like to be kept waiting."

"Shall I stand at attention until he arrives?" Ivy said, trying to mask a sudden wave of fear with sarcasm.

It was a wasted effort. Ivy could almost see the woman's raised eyebrows.

"His driver will come for you, Miss Madison, not the prince himself."

"Of course he won't," Ivy said, and hung up the phone.

Damian Aristedes was not a man who would sully his hands with work. Not even when it came to making arrangements about a woman.

His assistant probably did this kind of thing all the time. Fly one woman to Greece, fly another to Timbuktu… The prince would expect a mistress to be available on demand.

He was in for a big surprise.

She would never become his mistress. She would never agree to become his anything, much less his wife—although that, obviously, had been a lie. A little bait to lure her into his bed.

Not that he'd need bait for most women.

Put him in a room with a dozen women, all beautiful enough to get any man they wanted, he'd have to fight them off. All that macho. The aura of power. The beautiful, masculine face; the hard-bodied good looks…

The prince would collect lovers with disquieting ease.

But she would not be one of them.

Getting sexually involved with a man was not on the list of things Ivy wanted to do with her life. And if that ever changed—and she couldn't imagine that it would—she would choose someone who was Damian's opposite.

She'd want a lover who was gentle, not authoritative. Caring, not commanding. A man whose touch would be nonthreatening.

The prince's touch was not like that.

Each caress left her shaken. Trembling. Feeling as if she were standing on the edge of a precipice and one more step would send her plunging to the rocks below…

Or soaring into a hot, sun-bleached sky.

Ivy let out a breath. Enough of this. There was more than an hour to go until the prince's driver came for her.

Plenty of time to get ready. Too much time, really. The last thing she wanted was to think about what lay ahead.

Ivy brewed a cup of ginger tea. She sat in a corner of the wide windowsill, shivering a little in the cool dawn hours as she sipped her tea and wondered how long it would be until she sat here again.

Soon, she promised herself. Soon.

At seven, she packed, showered and dressed. She was ready long before Damian's driver rang the bell.

He was polite.

So was she.

The big Mercedes rolled silently through the busy Manhattan streets. Ivy looked out through the dark glass at people going about their everyday lives and wondered why she'd let this happen. She didn't have the money for a good attorney but she knew lots of people in high places. Surely someone could help her...

Then she remembered what had started all this. She had agreed to have this baby and Damian Aristedes was the child's father.

She had no choice but to do as he wished.

It was the right thing, for Kay's memory, for the baby...

"Miss?"

Ivy looked up. The car had stopped; the driver stood beside her open door.

"We're here, miss."

"Here" was a place she'd been before. Kennedy Airport, a part of it that was home to private jets.

She'd been a passenger in private planes going to and

from photo shoots in exotic locations. The planes were often big, but she'd never seen a noncommercial aircraft the size of the one ahead of her.

Sunlight glinted off the shiny aluminum wings, danced on the fuselage and the discreet logo emblazoned there. A shield. A lance. An animal of some kind, bulky and somehow dangerous, even in repose.

"Miss Madison?"

A courteous steward led her to the plane. He had that same logo on the pocket of his dark blue jacket and she realized it was a crest. A royal crest, for the royal house of Aristedes.

What are you doing, Ivy? What in the world are you doing?

She stumbled to a halt. The steward looked at her. So did Damian's driver, who was carrying her suitcase to the plane.

Someone else was looking at her, too, from inside the cabin. She couldn't see him but she knew he was there, watching her through cool eyes, seeing her hesitate, assessing it as a sign of weakness.

She would never show weakness to him!

Ivy took a breath and walked briskly up the steps that led into the plane.

It was cool inside the cabin. Luxurious, too. The walls were pale cream; the seats and small sofas soft-looking tan leather. Thick cream carpet stretched the length of the fuselage to a closed door in the rear.

And, yes, Damian was already there, sitting in one of the leather chairs, not looking at her but, instead, reading a page from the sheaf of papers stacked on the table in front of him.

"Miss Madison, sir," the steward said.

Damian raised his head.

Ivy stood straighter, automatically taking on the cool look she'd made famous in myriad ads and magazine covers.

She had deliberately taken time with her appearance this morning. At first, she'd thought she'd wear jeans and a ratty jacket she kept for solitary walks on chill winter mornings, just to show the prince how little all his wealth and grandeur meant.

She'd known, instinctively, he'd have a private plane. Men like him wouldn't fly in commercial jets.

Then she'd thought, no, far better to make it clear nothing he owned, nothing he was, could intimidate her. So she'd dressed in cashmere and silk under a glove-leather black jacket she'd picked up after a shoot in Milan the prior year.

She needn't have bothered.

Damian barely glanced at her, nodded curtly and went back to work.

It angered her, which was ridiculous. It was good, wasn't it, that he had no intention of pretending this was a social occasion?

She nodded back and started past him. His arm shot out, blocking her way.

"You will sit here," he said.

"Here" was the leather chair next to his.

"I prefer a seat further back."

"I don't recall asking your preference."

His tone was frigid. It made her want to slap his face but she wasn't fool enough to do that again. Far better to save her energy for the battles ahead, instead of wasting it on minor skirmishes.

Ivy sat down. The hovering steward cleared his throat.

"May I bring you something after we reach cruising altitude, madam? Coffee, perhaps, or tea?"

"No coffee," Damian said, without lifting his head. "No tea. No alcohol. Ms. Madison may have mineral water or juice, as she prefers."

Ivy felt her face flame. Why didn't he simply announce her pregnancy to the world? But if he was trying to lure her into all-out war, he was going to be disappointed.

"How nice," she said calmly, "to be given a choice, even if it's a minor one."

Damian looked up. Waited. His mouth gave a perfunctory twitch. "Should Thomas take that to mean you don't want anything?"

"What I want," she said matter-of-factly, "is my freedom, but I doubt if Thomas can provide that."

The steward's eyes widened. Damian's face darkened. For a second, no one moved or spoke. Then Damian broke the silence.

"That will be all, Thomas." He waited until the steward was gone. Then he turned to Ivy. "That is the last time I will tolerate that," he said in a low voice.

"Tolerate what, Your Highness? The truth?"

His hand closed on her wrist, exerting just enough pressure to make her gasp.

"You will show me the proper respect in front of people or—"

"Or what?"

His eyes narrowed. "Try me and find out."

A shudder went through her but she kept her gaze steadily on his until he finally let go of her, turned away and began reading through the papers spread in front of him again.

Ivy drew a deep, almost painful breath.

She would get through this. She'd survived worse. Far worse. Things that had happened long ago, that she wanted to forget but couldn't…

That had made her strong.

The mighty prince didn't know it, but he would learn just how strong she was.

When they were airborne, the steward, brave man, appeared with both juice and water as well as a stack of current magazines. Ivy thanked him, leafed through one and then another, blind to the glossy pages, thinking only about what lay ahead.

And about what Damian had said last night.

She'd refused to dwell on it then but now, after this display of power, his words haunted her.

From now on, he'd said, *I own you.*

She thought—she really thought he might believe it. That he had bought her. That she would go to his bed. That she would do whatever he commanded, become the perfect sex slave.

Let him kiss her breasts, as he had so shockingly done yesterday.

Let him undress her. Stand her, naked, before him.

Let him take her in his arms, gather her tightly against him while his aroused flesh pulsed against her.

Let him do all the things men did to women, things men wanted and women surely despised…except, she hadn't despised what Damian did last night.

When he'd touched her. Held her. Kissed her. Parted her lips with his…

Tasted her, let her taste him.

Ivy turned blindly to the window.

The baby. She had to think about the baby. That was all that mattered.

* * *

It grew dark outside the plane.

The cabin lights dimmed.

She yawned. Yawned again. Tumbled into darkness... And shot awake to see Damian leaning over her.

"What—what are you doing?"

His mouth twitched. She'd seen that little movement of his lips enough to know he was trying not to smile.

"Did you think I was going to ravish you while you slept?" This time, the smile he'd repressed broke through. "I'm not a fool, *glyka mou*. When I make love to you, I want you fully awake in my arms."

She was too tired to think of a clever response. Or maybe he was too close, his fallen angel's face an inch from hers.

"I was going to adjust your seat," he said softly. "So that you could lie back while you were sleeping."

"I wasn't sleeping."

"While you were resting, then," he said, with another of those heart-stopping little smiles. "Here. Let me—"

He leaned closer. All she had to do was turn her face a fraction of an inch and her mouth would find his.

Ivy jerked back. "Don't you ever get tired of giving orders?"

"Don't you ever get tired of ignoring good advice?" He shifted his weight. The little distance she'd put between them disappeared. "We have hours left before we land."

"So?"

"So, you're exhausted."

"And you know this, how? You read cards? Palms? Crystal balls?"

His smile tilted. "Unless I'm mistaken, you slept as little as I did last night."

She wanted to ask him why he hadn't slept. Was it because he was sorry he'd demanded she go with him? Or was it—was it because he'd lain in the dark, imagining what it would be like if they had made love? If, together, they'd made the baby growing inside her?

Did what she'd just thought show on her face? Was that why his eyes had suddenly darkened?

"And," he said, very softly, "you're pregnant."

Amazing. They had discussed her pregnancy in excruciating—if not entirely accurate—detail. Still, the way he said the word now, his husky whisper intimate and sexy, made her heartbeat stumble.

"I see. Now you're an expert on pregnant women." She spoke quickly, saying the first thing that came into her head in a desperate effort to defuse the situation, and knew in an instant she'd made a mistake.

A mask seemed to drop over his face.

"What little I know about pregnancy," he said, drawing away from her, "comes courtesy of Kay. Your sister used endless ploys to convince me she was carrying my child."

"Kay wasn't my real sister," Ivy said, and wondered why it suddenly seemed important he understand that.

"Yes. You said you were stepsisters. The same last name... Then, your mother married her father and he adopted you?"

Why had she brought this up? "Yes."

"How old were you?"

"It's not important."

She turned away from him but he cupped her jaw, his touch firm but light.

"I have the right to know these things."

She supposed he did. And he could learn them easily enough. Anything more than that, she had no intention of sharing.

"I was ten. Kay was fourteen."

"She told me her father died when she was sixteen. Another lie?"

"No." Ivy laced her hands in her lap. "He died two years after my mother married him. They both died, he and my mother. It was a freak accident, a helicopter crash in Hawaii. They were on vacation, on a tour."

"I am sorry, *glyka mou.* That must have been hard for you."

She nodded.

"So, who took care of you then? What happened?"

Everything, Ivy thought, oh God, everything...

"Nothing," she said airily. "Well, Kay and I went into foster care. When she turned eighteen, she got a job and a place of her own."

"And you went with her?"

"No." Ivy bit her lip. "I stayed in foster care."

"And?"

And my world changed, forever.

But she didn't say that. Her life was none of his business, and that was exactly what she told him.

"The only part of my life that concerns you," she said sharply, "is my pregnancy."

Ivy expected one of those cold commands that were his specialty or, at least, an argument. Instead, to her surprise, Damian gave her a long, questioning look. Then he turned away and pressed the call button.

The steward appeared as quickly as if he were conjured up from Aladdin's lamp.

"We would like dinner now, Thomas," Damian said. "Broiled salmon. Green salad with oil and vinegar. Baked potatoes."

"Of course, Your Highness."

He was doing it again. Thinking for her. Speaking about her as if she were incapable of speaking for herself. It made her angry and that was good.

Anger was a safer emotion than whatever Damian had made her feel a little while ago.

"I'm not hungry," Ivy said sharply.

Nobody answered. Nobody even looked at her.

"I'll have a glass of Riesling first, Thomas. And please bring Ms. Madison some Perrier and lemon."

"I do not want—"

"No lemon in the Perrier? Of course. No lemon, Thomas. *Neh?*"

"Certainly, sir."

Ivy smoldered but kept silent until they were alone. Then she swung angrily toward Damian, who was calmly putting the documents he'd been reading into a leather briefcase.

"Do you have a hearing problem? I said I wasn't hungry!"

"You are eating for two."

"That's outmoded nonsense!"

"If you are vain enough to wish to starve yourself—"

"I am not starving myself!"

"*Ŏhi,*" Damian said evenly. "That is correct. You are not. I will not permit it."

"Damn it," Ivy snarled, letting her anger rise, embracing it, reminding herself that she hated this man, that it would be dangerous to let any other emotion come into play where he was concerned, "I don't even understand what you're saying. Since when does 'no' mean 'yes' and 'okay' mean 'no'?"

He looked blank. Then he chuckled. "It's not 'no,' it's *'neh.'* It means 'yes.' And I didn't say 'okay,' I said *ŏhi,* which means 'no.'"

Yes was no. No was yes. Would a white rabbit pop out of the carpet next?

"I shall arrange for a tutor to teach you your new language, *glyka mou.*"

"My language is English," she said, despising the petulance in her own voice.

"Your new home is Greece."

"No. It isn't. My home is the place you took me from. That will always be my home, and I'll never let you forget it." She glared at him, her breath coming quickly, furious at him, at herself, at what was happening, what she had brought down on herself. "And if you really think I'd starve myself and hurt my baby—"

"My baby," he said coldly, all the ease of the last moments gone. "Not yours."

The true answer, the one she longed to give him, feared to give him, danced on the tip of her tongue. He claimed he hadn't loved Kay, but Kay had sworn he had. There were too many lies, too many layers of them to risk the one truth that might tear the whole web asunder.

Far too much risk.

So Ivy bit back what she'd come close to saying. Damian filled the silence with yet another order.

"You will eat properly. And you will not contradict me in front of my people. Is that clear?"

"Do I have to genuflect in your presence, too?"

No telltale twitch of his lips this time, only a cold glare.

"If you feel you must, by all means, do so."

He turned away. So did she. There seemed nothing more to say.

They ate in silence.

Ivy tried to pretend disinterest in her food but she was ravenous. Had she eaten anything since her first confrontation with Damian? She couldn't remember.

The steward cleared their tables and brought dessert. Two crystal flutes filled with fresh strawberries, topped with a dollop of cream. She could, at least, make a stand here.

"I never eat whipped cream," she said with lofty determination.

"I'm happy to hear it because this is crème fraîche."

Hadn't she promised herself she wouldn't try to fight him on little things? Crème fraîche was absolutely a little thing, wasn't it?

Little, and delicious. She ate every berry, every bit of the cream…

And felt Damian's gaze on her.

His eyes—hot, intense, almost black with passion— were riveted to her mouth as she licked the last bit from the spoon.

A wave of heat engulfed her; a choked sound broke from her throat. He heard it, lifted his gaze to hers…

The cabin door slid open. Thomas appeared, looked quickly from his master to Ivy…

Ivy sprang to her feet. "Where's the—where is the lavatory, please?"

"In the back, miss. I can show you…"

"I can find it myself, thank you," she said.

And fled.

* * *

They were flying through a black sky lit by a sliver of ivory moon.

Damian had the light on. There were papers in his lap but he wasn't looking at them. Ivy had a magazine in hers but she wasn't looking at it, either.

She was trying to stay awake. Trying to stay awake…

To her horror, she gave a jaw-creaking yawn.

"If you were tired," Damian said coolly, "which, of course, you are not, you could recline your seat and close your eyes."

She went on ignoring him. And yawned. Yawned again…

Her eyelids drooped. A minute, that was all she needed. Just a minute with her eyes shut…

She jerked upright. Her head was on Damian's shoulder. Flustered, she pulled away.

"You are the most stubborn woman in the world. Damn it, what will you prove by not sleeping?"

"I told you, I'm not—"

"Oh, for heaven's sake…" His arm closed around her shoulders. She protested; he ignored her and drew her to his side. "Close your eyes."

"You can't order someone to—"

"Yes," he said firmly, "I can." His arm tightened around her. "Go to sleep." His tone softened. "I promise, I'll keep you safe."

Safe? How could she feel safe in the embrace of this imperious stranger?

And yet—and yet, she did. Feel safe. Warm. Content to lean her head against his hard shoulder. To feel the soft brush of his lips on her temple.

Strong arms closed around her. Lifted her, carried her

through the dark cabin. Lay her down gently on a wide, soft bed.

Was she dreaming?

"Yes," a husky voice whispered, "you are dreaming. Why not give yourself up to the dream?"

It wasn't a dream. The bed was real. The voice was Damian's. And she was in Damian's arms, her body pressed to the length of his.

"I won't sleep with you," she heard herself whisper.

He gave a soft laugh. "You are sleeping with me right now, *glyka mou*," he whispered back, though that term he used for her, whatever it meant, sounded somehow different. Softer. Sweeter…

Sweet as the whisper of his mouth over hers, again and again until she sighed and let her lips cling to his for one quick, transcendent moment.

"You are killing me, *glyka mou*," he said thickly. "But sleep is all we'll share tonight." Another kiss, another gruff whisper. "I want you wide-awake when we make love."

"Never," Ivy heard herself whisper.

She felt his lips curve against hers in a smile.

"Go to sleep," he said.

After that, there was only darkness.

CHAPTER SEVEN

IN THE earliest hours of the morning, Damian's plane landed on his private airstrip on Minos.

The intercom light blinked on; the machine gave a soft beep. "We have arrived, Your Highness," the steward's voice said politely.

"*Efharisto,* Thomas."

Ivy didn't stir. She'd been asleep in Damian's arms for almost two hours, her head tucked into the curve of his shoulder.

By now, his shoulder ached but he wouldn't have moved her for anything in the world.

How could sleeping with a woman, sleeping with her in the most literal sense of the word, feel so wonderful?

Damian turned his head, breathing in Ivy's scent. Silky strands of her hair brushed against his lips. He closed his eyes and thought about staying here with her, just like this, until she awakened.

Impossible, of course.

They had to return to reality eventually. It might as well be now.

But he could wake her quietly. Show her that every moment they were together didn't have to be a battle.

Gently he rolled her onto her back, bent to her and kissed her.

"*Kalimera*," said softly.

Ivy sighed and he kissed her again.

"Ivy," he whispered. "Wake up. We're home."

Her lashes fluttered open to reveal eyes were dark, still clouded with sleep.

"Damian?"

His name was soft on her lips. She'd never spoken it that way before, as if he and she were alone in the universe.

"Yes, it's me, sweetheart. Did you sleep well?"

"I don't—I don't remember. How did we…?"

Her eyes widened and he knew she'd realized she was not only in his arms but in his bed. He'd watched Lucas taming a mare once; that same wild look had come into the animal's eyes.

"Easy," he said.

"What am I doing in this bed?"

"Sleeping. Nothing more than that."

"But—how did I get here? I don't remember…"

"I carried you. You were exhausted."

She closed her eyes. When she opened them again, they were cool. "Let me up."

"In a minute."

"Damian—"

"Do you see what sleeping in my arms has accomplished?" He smiled. "You've begun calling me Damian."

She started to answer. He kissed her instead. She didn't respond. But he went on kissing her, his mouth moving lightly over hers, and just when he thought it would never happen, she sighed and parted her lips to his.

The joining of their mouths was tender.

The need that swept through him was not.

His erection was instantaneous and he groaned and shifted his weight to accommodate the ache of his hardened flesh. Ivy shifted, too…and he found himself cradled between her parted thighs.

She gasped into his mouth.

His blood thundered.

Now, it said, take her now…

Beep. "Sir? Will you be deplaning, or shall I tell the pilot to leave the electrical system on?"

That was all it took to destroy the fragile moment. Ivy tore her mouth from Damian's. Her face was flushed, her lips full and heated from his kisses. He wanted to cup her face, kiss her into submission…

Instead he rolled away and rose from the bed. She did, too, but as she got to her feet, he scooped her into his arms.

"I can walk."

"It's dark outside."

"I can see."

"I know the terrain. You don't."

A Jeep and driver waited on the side of the runway. His driver was well-trained. Either that, or the arrival of his employer with a woman in his arms was not an unusual event.

Ivy was not as casual. She saw the driver and buried her face in Damian's throat.

The feel of her mouth on his skin, the warmth of her breath… He loved it almost as much as the feel of her in his arms during the short drive to his palace, perched on the ancient, long-dormant volcanic summit of Minos.

The palace was lit softly in anticipation of his arrival. He wondered what Ivy would think of his home when she saw it tomorrow by daylight. He'd learned that most people envisioned a palace as an imposing edifice of stone.

His home, if you could call a palace a home, was built of marble. The oldest part of it dated to the fourth century, another wing to the sixth, and the balance to the early 1600s. It was an enormous, sprawling, overblown place...

But he loved it.

Would Ivy? Not that it mattered, of course, but if she lived here with him, if, after his son's birth, she became his—she became his—

The huge bronze doors swung open, revealing his houseman, Esias. Despite the hour, Esias was formally dressed.

Damian had given up trying to break him of the habit. Esias had served his grandfather, his father and now him. How could you argue with an icon—an icon who was as determined as the Jeep's driver not to show surprise at seeing his master with a woman in his arms.

"Welcome home, Your Highness."

"Esias."

"May I, ah, may I help you with—"

"I am fine, thank you."

"Damian," Ivy snapped. "My God, put me—"

"Soon."

Trailed by Esias, he carried her up a wide, curving marble staircase to the second floor, then down the corridor that led to his rooms.

Esias stepped forward and opened the door.

"*Efharisto,*" Damian said. "That is all, Esias. I'll see you in the morning."

The houseman inclined his head and moved back. Damian carried Ivy through the door and shouldered it shut, and the silence of the room closed around them.

"Who was that?"

He was alone with his mistress and the first words out of her mouth were not the ones a man ached to hear…

But then, Ivy wasn't his mistress.

Not yet.

"Damian. Who was—"

He answered by kissing her. She tried to turn her face away but he was persistent. He kept kissing her, nipped gently at her bottom lip and, at last, she made a little sound and opened her mouth to his.

He slipped the tip of his tongue between her parted lips. She jerked back. Then she made that sweet little whisper again and accepted the intimate caress. Accepted and returned it as he carried her through the sitting room, through the bedroom, to his bed.

Pleasure coursed through him.

What had happened in the darkness of the plane had changed everything. Had she realized she couldn't fight him or herself? That she wanted him as much as he wanted her?

God knew, he wanted her. From the minute she'd turned up at his door, despite everything, his anger, hell, his rage…

No woman had ever stirred such hunger in him.

Gently he lay her down in the silk-covered bed. Moonlight, streaming through the French doors behind it, touched her hair with silver. Her eyes, brighter than the stars, glittered as she looked up at him.

"Ivy," he said softly. He bent to her. Kissed her

temples. Her mouth. Her throat. Whispered in Greek what he would do to her, with her…

What she would feel as he made her his.

"Damian?"

Her whisper was soft. Uncertain. It had an innocence to it that he knew was a lie but it suited the way she was looking at him, the way her hands had come up to press lightly against his chest.

A little game could be exciting, though she excited him enough just as she was. He was almost painfully hard. It would not be easy to go as slowly as he wanted, this first time, but he would try.

Her dress had a row of tiny buttons down the bodice. He undid them slowly, even as her hands caught at his, and he paused to kiss each bit of warm, rosy skin he exposed.

She was breathing fast; the glitter in her eyes had become almost feverish.

"Damian," she whispered. "Please…"

He kissed her, harder this time, deeper, and she moved against him. Yes God, yes. Like that. Just like that…

Her bra opened in the front. He sent up a silent prayer of thanks as he undid the clasp, let the silk cups fall open…

And groaned.

She was exquisite.

She had small, perfect breasts crowned by pale pink nipples. It had almost driven him insane, touching them that one time…

"Damian! Stop."

She was moving against him again. It was too much. If she kept lifting herself to him this way, he would—

"Stop!"

He didn't hear her. Or yes, he heard her voice but her words had no meaning as he drew one nipple deep into his mouth—

Something slammed into his chest. He jerked back. It was Ivy's fist; even as he watched, she swung at him again. Stunned, he grabbed her wrists.

"What the hell are you doing?"

"Get—off—me!"

She was crying. And yes, moving against him, not in passion but in an attempt to free herself of his weight.

He sat up, stunned, disbelieving. She scrambled away from him and shot to her feet, clutching the open bodice of her dress, staring at him as if he were a monster.

"Don't touch me!"

"Don't touch you? But—"

"I told you I didn't want to come here. I told you I would not be your—your sex toy. And now—now, the minute we're alone in this—this kingdom you rule, you start—you start pawing me."

Pawing her? She had clung to him. Kissed him. Looked into his eyes with desire and now...

And now, it was time to up the ante. Make the game more interesting because she knew damned well he could always toss in his cards and walk away from the table.

He wanted to throw her back down on the rumpled bed, pin her arms over her head, force her thighs apart and finish what she had started, but she would not reduce him to that.

For all he knew, that was exactly what she wanted.

He snarled a name at her, one he'd never called any

woman. Then he turned on his heel, strode through the suite, into the hall and slammed the door behind him.

Lucas had called it right. First Kay had played him for a sucker. Now Ivy was doing it. And he, fool that he was, had let it happen.

She was only a woman. A pretty face, a ripe body. God knew, there were plenty of those in his life. Yes, she carried his child but he knew damned well she hadn't done it out of love for her sister.

She'd done it for money. Lots of it, probably. And then fate had intervened, taken Kay out of the picture, and Ivy would have seen that whatever Kay had promised her could be increased a hundredfold, a thousandfold, if she played the game right.

The lock clicked.

Panagia mou! She had locked the door against him. Locked *his* door against him. To hell with that. If she thought he'd put up with such crap, she needed to learn a lesson.

Starting right now.

He took a step back, aimed his foot at the door…

"Sir?"

Damian whirled around. "Get the hell out of here, Esias!"

His houseman stood his ground, no emotion showing on his face as if it were perfectly normal to find his master about to kick down the door of his own sitting room.

"I am sorry to disturb you, Your Highness, but your office in Athens is trying to reach you. They say it is urgent."

Esias held out the telephone. Damian glared at it. What did he give a damn for his office in Athens? Except—except, it was the middle of the night.

The bitch laughing at him behind that door was only one woman. He could deal with her at his leisure. But if there was a problem in Athens, it could affect the hundreds of people who worked for him.

He held out his hand and Esias gave him the phone.

An Aristedes supertanker had run aground on a reef in South America. Oil might begin oozing into the ocean at any moment.

Damian tossed the phone to Esias. "Wake my pilot," he snapped. "Tell him—"

"I have taken the liberty of doing so. The helicopter will be ready when you get there."

"Thank you."

"You are welcome, Your Highness." The houseman paused and looked at the closed door. "Ah, is there anything else, sir?"

"Yes," Damian said coldly. "The lady's name is Ivy Madison. Make her comfortable, but under no circumstances is she to leave this island."

Two days later, the crisis in South America had been resolved and Damian was on his way back to Minos.

It had been a hard, exhausting couple of days but it had given him time to calm down.

If he hadn't been called away…

No, he thought, staring at the ocean swells far below the fast-moving helicopter, no, he wouldn't think about that. Ivy had deliberately taken him to the brink of self-control.

He was certain of it.

But he hadn't let her push him over the edge. And there was no chance it would happen again.

Two days in Athens. Two days away from temptation.

Two days of rational thought and he'd come to a decision.

He'd made a mistake, bringing her to Minos. As for the rest, telling her he'd make her his mistress, that he might marry her...

Damian shook his head. Crazy. Or perhaps crazed was a better way to put it.

Why would he have even considered making her his mistress? All the emotional baggage that went into an arrangement like that? No way. The world was full of beautiful women. He surely didn't need this particular one.

As for marriage... Crazy, for sure. He wasn't marrying anybody. Not for years to come, if at all. And when that time came, assuming it did, *he* would choose his own wife, not let her choose him.

Because that was what had been going on. How come he hadn't seen it right away?

Like her sister, Ivy had been angling for marriage from the start. She was just cleverer about it. An ambush, instead of a head-on attack. That way, the target didn't stand a chance.

Her weapon had been the oldest one in the world. Sex. What could be more powerful in the hands of a beautiful woman, especially if a man was vulnerable?

And he sure as hell was vulnerable. He hadn't had a woman for months. Damian's jaw tightened. But he would, very soon.

Late last night, once he was sure the South American situation was under control, he'd phoned a French actress he'd met a few weeks ago. A couple of minutes of conversation and the upshot was, he'd fly to Paris next weekend.

She was looking forward to it, she'd purred.

So was he.

A long weekend in bed with the actress and Ivy would be forgotten. Hell, he'd forgotten her already...

"Your Highness?"

How long had the pilot's voice been buzzing in his headset? Damian cleared his throat.

"Yes?"

"Touchdown in a couple of minutes, sir."

"Thank you."

They were flying lower now, skimming over a group of small islands that were part of the Cyclades, as was Minos, but these bits of land were uninhabited, as beautiful as they were wild.

Back in the days he'd had time for such things, he'd sailed a Sunfish here and explored them. Sometimes, making his way through the tall pines that clung to them, he'd half expected to come face-to-face with one of the ancient gods his people had once worshipped.

Or one of the goddesses. Aphrodite. Artemis. Helen of Troy. Not a goddess, no, but a woman whose beauty had brought a man to his knees.

Ivy had almost done that to him, but fate had intervened.

A man could come to his senses, given breathing room.

The helicopter settled onto its landing pad. Damian slapped the pilot on the shoulder with his thanks and got out, automatically ducking under the whirring blades as he ran to the Jeep, parked where he'd left it two nights ago. It was six in the morning. He was tired, unshaven and he couldn't recall when he'd showered last. Added to that, he was hungry enough to eat shoe leather.

But all that would wait. Dealing with Ivy was more important. He wanted her off his island, and fast.

Yes, he thought, as the Jeep bounced along the narrow road, she was carrying his child. And yes, she needed watching. He knew that, better than before.

But he didn't have to be the one doing the watching. She'd said that herself. Of course, he knew now that she hadn't said it in hopes he'd listen. Just the opposite: she'd wanted to lure him into doing exactly what he'd done.

The funny thing was, it might have been the one true thing to come out of her mouth.

That soft, beautiful, treacherous mouth.

Damn it, what did that have to do with anything? Who gave a damn about her mouth or any other part of her anatomy except her womb?

He'd contact his lawyers. Have them make arrangements to set her up in a place of her own. Have them organize round-the-clock coverage of her and her apartment.

Until his son was born, he would regulate who she saw, what she did, every breath she took. But not in New York City.

Damian smiled coldly as he took the Jeep through a hairpin turn.

He'd keep a watch on her from a much closer vantage point.

Athens.

She would give birth here, in his country, where his peoples' laws, where his nationality and his considerable leverage, would apply.

She wouldn't like it—and that, he had to admit, was part of the reason the plan gave him so much pleasure.

* * *

He entered the palace through a secret door some ancestor had added in the fifteenth century so he could spy on a cheating wife, or so the story went.

He had no desire to go through the usual polite morning moves— *Good morning, sir. Good morning, Esias.* Or Elena, or Jasper, or Aeneas, or any of the half dozen others on the household staff.

The only person he wanted to see was Ivy. He'd ring for a cup of coffee. Then he'd have her brought to him so he could tell her what would happen next.

She'd moved into one of the guest suites. Esias had phoned to tell him that within an hour of his reaching his office. It had been well before he'd come to his senses and, for a wild moment, he'd imagined returning to Minos, storming into her suite, tumbling her back on the bed and finishing what had started before he'd had to leave for Athens.

Thank God, he hadn't.

He didn't want to carry through on the threat he'd made in New York, either. He didn't want to own her, only to get rid of her. So what if, despite his newfound sanity, he could still remember the smell of her skin? The sweetness of her mouth? The taste of her nipples?

Damian stopped halfway up the stairs. Stop it, he told himself angrily. There was nothing special about Ivy. Another few days and he'd be with a woman who would not play games, who would not stir him to frustration and madness.

Who wouldn't sigh the way Ivy did, when he kissed her. Or whisper his name as if it were music. Or fall asleep in his arms, as if he were keeping her safe…

"Damn it, Aristedes," he said under his breath, and opened the door to his suite…

And saw Ivy, standing with her back to him…

Waiting for him.

His heart turned over, and he knew everything he'd told himself the last two days were lies.

The truth was, he wanted this woman more than he wanted his next breath—and she wanted him, too. Why else would she be here, waiting for his return?

He said her name and she swung to face him. His heart began to race. There was no artifice in her expression. Whatever she told him next would be the truth.

"Damian. You're here."

"Yes," he said softly, "and so are you."

"I—I heard the helicopter. And—and I went downstairs and asked Esias if you were coming and he said—he said yes, you were returning to Minos. And when he told me that, I felt—"

She was hurrying the words, rushing them together and he understood. It wouldn't be easy to admit she'd been teasing him, that the teasing was over.

"You don't have to explain."

"But I do. I owe you that. I know—I know you think what I did the other night—that I did it deliberately, but—"

He closed the distance between them, caught her wrists and brought her hands to his lips.

"It was a game. I understand. But it's over with. No more games, Ivy. From now on, we'll be honest with each other, *neh?*"

She nodded. "Yes. Absolutely honest."

Damian brought her hands to his chest. "Let me shower. Then we'll have some breakfast. And then—"

His voice roughened. "And then, sweetheart, I'll show you how much I want you. How good it will be when we make love."

Ivy jerked her hands from his. "What?"

He grinned. "You're right. No breakfast. Just a quick shower…" His gaze dropped to her mouth, then rose again. "You can shower with me," he whispered. "Would you like that?"

"You have no idea what I'm talking about!"

"I do, *kardia mou*. You want to apologize for—"

"Apologize?" Her voice rose in disbelief. "Apologize? For what?"

"For the other night," he said carefully. "For teasing me—"

"Teasing you?" She stared at him; for a second, he wondered if he were speaking Greek instead of English. "Are you crazy?"

Damian's mouth narrowed. "It would seem that one of us is."

"You—you tried to take advantage of me the other night. And now—now, my God, you're so full of yourself that you think—that you think… Do you really think I waited here to beg you to take me to bed?" Ivy lifted her hand and poked her forefinger into the center of his chest. "I waited here to tell you that I am going home!"

"You came to my rooms, waited for me, all so you could tell me you're leaving Minos?"

Damian's voice was low and ugly. It made Ivy's heart leap.

Nothing was going the way she'd planned.

She'd expected him to be sharp with her. That would be her cue to tell him that it was illogical for them to spend the next six months in lock-step. What had happened the other night was proof they couldn't get along.

Why torture each other when it wasn't necessary?

She would go home. And she would agree to give him visiting rights to his son.

That was what she'd intended to tell him, but Damian had misunderstood everything. She'd waited in his rooms because she wanted this meeting to be private. She'd approached him in a conciliatory fashion because getting him angry would serve no purpose.

It had all backfired, and now he was looking at her the way a spider would look at a fly.

All right. She'd try again.

"Perhaps I should explain why I waited for you here."

"There's no need. I know the reason."

"I did it because—"

"Because you thought, perhaps I overplayed my hand. Perhaps my performance the other night convinced him to get rid of me."

"It wasn't a performance!"

"And then, because you're so very clever, so very good at this, you thought, yes, but if I say it first, if I tell him I want to leave, it will probably make him anxious to keep me."

"You're wrong! I never—"

She cried out as he caught hold of her and lifted her to her toes.

"The stakes are higher now, *neh?* Whatever Kay promised you as payment for your role in this ugly scheme—"

"She didn't promise me anything!"

"Perhaps not. Perhaps you thought to wait until my

son was in my arms before you asked for money." His fingers bit into her flesh. "But fate dealt you a better card."

"Can't you get it through your thick skull that not everything is about you?"

"You're wrong. This is all about me. My fortune. My title." His mouth twisted. "And the sweetener you keep dangling in front of my nose."

Before she could pull away, he kissed her, savaging her mouth, forcing her head back. Ivy stood immobile. Then memory and fear overwhelmed her and she sank her teeth into his lip.

He jerked back, tasting blood.

Slowly, deliberately, he wiped it away with the back of his hand.

"Be careful, *glyka mou*. My patience is wearing thin."

"You can't do this!"

"You are in my country. I can do anything I damned well please."

He let go of her, picked up the nearest telephone and punched a key.

"Esias. I want Ms. Madison's things moved to my rooms. Yes. Immediately."

Damian broke the connection and looked at Ivy. She stood straight and tall, head up, eyes steady on his even though they blazed with rage.

She was magnificent, so beautiful the sight of her made the blood roar in his ears.

He could take her now. Teach her that she belonged to him. Turn all that frost to flame.

But he wouldn't. The longer he waited, the sweeter her submission would be.

Damian strolled into the huge master bath. Turned on the shower, toed off his mocs, unbuckled his belt, pulled his cotton sweater over his head as if he were alone.

A priceless vase whistled past his ear and shattered on the tile a couple of feet away.

He swung around and looked at Ivy. She glared back, head high, hands on hips, her eyes telling him how she despised him...

And then her gaze dropped to his broad shoulders, swept over his muscled chest and hard abs.

"Want to see more?" he said, very softly, and brought his hand to his zipper.

His Ivy was brave but she wasn't stupid. Cheeks blazing, she turned and fled.

CHAPTER EIGHT

TRAPPED.

She was trapped like a fly in amber, Ivy thought furiously, held captive within something that looked beautiful but was really a prison.

The door to the guest suite she'd commandeered in Damian's absence stood open. One of the maids was emptying the dresser drawers; Esias stood by, supervising.

"Leave my clothes alone!"

The maid jumped back. Esias said something and the girl shot a glance at Ivy and reached toward the dresser again.

"Did you hear me? Do—not—touch—my—things!"

Esias barely looked at her. "His Highness said—"

"I don't give a damn what he said." Ivy pointed to the door. "Get out!"

The houseman stiffened but, well-trained robot that he was, he snapped an order at the maid. She scurried away at his heels as he marched from the room.

Ivy slammed the door behind them, locked it and sank down on the edge of the bed.

She would not remain on Minos. That was a given.

What wasn't so clear was how to escape. There were no bars on the windows of Damian's palace, no locks on the doors, but why would there be?

The island was in the middle of the Aegean. You could only leave it by sea or by air.

And yes, there was an airstrip, a helipad, a couple of small boats in a curved harbor, even a yacht the size of a cruise ship anchored just offshore in the dark blue sea.

But all those things, every ounce of white sand beach, dark volcanic rock and thousand-foot-high cliffs belonged to Damian. He owned Minos and ruled it with an iron fist.

She could only leave Minos if he permitted it.

Aside from Esias, who watched her with the intensity of Cerberus, that ancient three-headed dog guarding Hades, the people who lived in Damian's tightly controlled little kingdom were pleasant and polite.

The maids and gardeners, cook and housekeeper all smiled whenever they saw her. The pilot of Damian's jet, poring over charts in a small, whitewashed building at the airstrip, had greeted her pleasantly; down by the sea, an old man scraping barnacles from the bottom-up hull of a small sailboat doffed his cap and offered a gap-toothed grin.

They all spoke English, enough to say oh, yes, it was very hot this time of year and indeed, the sea was a wonderful shade of deepest blue. But as soon as Ivy even hinted at asking if someone would please sail her, fly her, get her the hell off this miserable speck of rock, they scratched their heads and suddenly lost their command of anything other than Greek.

Terrified, all of them, by His Highness, the Prince.

His Horribleness, the Prince.

Ivy shot to her feet and went to the closet. There had to be someone with the courage to help her. Maybe the helicopter pilot. Maybe Damian had neglected to tell him that she was a prisoner. Either way, this was her last chance at freedom.

She had to make it work and the best way to do that was to look and sound like Ivy Madison, woman of the world, instead of Ivy Madison, desperate prisoner.

Quickly she stripped to her bra and panties. Grabbed a pair of white linen trousers from their hanger, stepped into them…

"Oh, for God's sake…"

She inhaled until it felt like her navel was touching her spine. No good. The zipper wouldn't budge.

Ivy kicked the trousers off and turned sideways to the mirror. Her expression softened and she lay her hand gently over her rounded belly.

The baby—her baby—was growing. Her baby… and Damian's.

No. A condom's worth of semen didn't make a man a father. Concern, love, wanting a child were what mattered. Where was Damian's concern, his love, his desire for this baby?

Nowhere that she could see. He wanted her child because he wanted an heir, and because he was the kind of unfeeling SOB who could not imagine giving up that which he believed was his.

A man like that was not going to raise her baby.

Two days out from under his autocratic thumb and Ivy had had time to think logically.

Maybe she couldn't afford a five hundred dollar an hour Manhattan lawyer but she knew people who knew people. It was one of the few benefits of a high-profile career. Surely some acquaintance could fast-talk a hotshot attorney into taking her case on the cheap, maybe even pro bono, if only for the publicity.

Which was really pretty funny, Ivy thought as she tried and discarded another pair of trousers.

She'd always avoided publicity. Sometimes she thought she was the only model who tried to keep her private life under wraps. But if winning the right to raise her child alone meant having her face plastered in the papers, she'd do it.

She'd do whatever it took to get Damian out of her and her baby's lives.

Damian Aristedes was a brute. A monster. A man who went into a rage when he was denied sex, who'd come close to forcing her to yield to him and, instead, had flown to Athens to find a woman who wouldn't stop him from taking what he wanted.

Why else would he have left her and Minos? That was what men did. Even Damian, who looked so civilized.

He hadn't been civilized when he'd taken her in his arms the other night. Neither had she. Just for a moment, she'd felt things threaten to spin out of control... Until she'd come to her senses, realized where things were heading, what he would want to do next...

Ivy blinked, reached for the only remaining pair of trousers, sucked in her tummy and pulled them on.

Okay.

The zipper didn't close but at least it went up halfway. A long silk T, a loose, gauzy shirt over that...

She stuck her feet into a pair of high-heeled slides. Freed her hair from its clip, bent at the waist and ran her hands through it before tossing it back from her face. A little makeup…

Ivy looked at herself in the mirror, gave her reflection her best camera pout and tried to imagine herself facing the helicopter pilot, whoever he was.

"I know you must be awfully busy," she said in a breathy whisper. It made her want to gag when she heard other women talk like that but whatever worked… "I mean, I know you have lots to do…"

And what if the sexy look, the artful smile didn't budge him? If he said sorry, he had to clear it with the prince?

"Oh," she said, "yes, I know, but—but…" Ivy chewed on her lip. "But I have to get to Athens without telling him because—because—"

Because what?

"Because I want to buy him a gift. See, it's a surprise but it won't be if he knows about it…"

Not great but add a smile, fluttering lashes, maybe a light touch on the guy's arm…

Ivy's sexy smile faded.

"Yuck," she said.

Then she propped her sunglasses on top of her head, hung her purse over her shoulder and got moving.

The helicopter was still on its pad.

Better still, a guy wearing a ball cap and dark glasses was squatting alongside it, examining one of the struts.

It had to be the pilot.

Ivy paused, ran her hand through her hair, then down her torso. She was dusty and sweaty, thanks to the long walk to the helipad, plus she'd come close to turning her ankle on the road's gravel surface. There were Jeeps garaged near the palace but you had to get keys from Esias.

Fat chance.

Besides, some men liked sweaty. All those times she'd had to be oiled before a shot…

"Stop stalling," she muttered as she walked past the hangars, placing one foot directly ahead of the other.

Her modeling strut had always been among the best.

She waited until she was a couple of yards away. "Hi."

The guy looked up, gave a very satisfactory double-take and got to his feet.

Ivy held out her hand. "I'm Ivy."

He wiped his hand on his khakis, took her hand and cleared his throat. "Joe," he said, and cleared his throat again.

"Joe." Ivy batted her lashes. "Are you the one who flies this incredible thing?"

He grinned. "You got it, beautiful."

Perfect. He was American. And even with dust on her shoes and sweat beaded above her lip, she'd clearly passed the test.

"Well, Joe, I need a lift to Athens. Are you up for that?"

Joe took off his dark glasses, maybe so she could see the regret in his eyes, and peered past her.

"Are you, uh, are you looking for somebody?"

He nodded. "I'm looking for the prince."

"Oh, we don't need him." Ivy moved closer. "You see," she said, lowering her voice and gazing up at Joe's face, "he doesn't know I'm doing this."

She launched into her story. It sounded so good, she almost believed it. Joe said "uh huh" and "sure" and "cool." And just when she thought she had it made, he shook his head and sighed.

"Wish I could help you, beautiful, but I can't."

Ivy forced a smile. "But you can. I mean, it's just a little trip. And afterward, when the prince knows about the surprise, you know, after I've given it to him, I'll tell him how great you were, how you did this for me—"

"Sorry, babe. This chopper doesn't leave the ground unless His Highness says it's okay. You want to use the phone in the office over there to call him, that's fine. Otherwise—"

"For heaven's sake! Do you need his permission to breathe, too? You're a grown man. He's just a—he's just a pompous, self-serving—"

Joe stared past her, eyes widening.

"Glyka mou," a husky voice purred, "here you are."

Ivy's heart sank. She closed her eyes as a powerful arm wrapped around her shoulders.

"I've been looking everywhere for you. How foolish of me not to have thought to check here first."

Ivy looked up at Damian. He smiled, pleasantly enough so the pilot smiled, too, but Ivy wasn't fooled.

Behind that calm royal smile was hot royal rage.

"You cannot do this," she hissed.

His eyebrows rose. "Do what?"

"You know what. Refuse to let me leave. Make me into your—your—"

He bent his head and kissed her, the curve of his arm anchoring her to him while his mouth moved against hers with slow, possessive deliberation. She heard Joe clear his throat, heard her heart start to pound.

And felt herself tumble into the flood of dark sensation that came whenever his lips touched hers.

"I hate you," she whispered when he finally lifted his head.

His smile was one part sex and one part macho smirk. "Yes," he said. "I can tell. Joe?"

The pilot, who'd walked several feet away, turned to them. "Sir?"

"We are ready to leave," Damian said, and he took Ivy's elbow and all but lifted her into the helicopter.

They flew to Athens.

Even in her anger, Ivy felt a little thrill of excitement as they swooped over a stand of soaring white columns. She'd been to Athens before but it had been on business, four rushed days and nights of being photographed with no time for anything else except a hurried visit to the Parthenon.

Was that the Acropolis below them now? She wanted to ask but not if it meant speaking to Damian.

She didn't have to. He leaned in close, put his lips to her ear and told her what was beneath them.

The whisper of his breath made her tremble. Why? How could she hate him and yet react this way to him? To any man? She knew what they were, what they wanted...

"I should have thought to ask," he said. "Is the flight making you ill?"

Ivy pulled away. "Not the flight," she said coldly, but he didn't hear her, couldn't hear her over the roar of the engine, and that was just as well.

His show of concern was just that. A show, nothing more. She was his captive and that was how he treated her and why in God's name did she respond to his touch?

He must have had the same effect on Kay. Otherwise, she wouldn't have given in to his demands. The bastard! Forcing Kay to do what he wanted, then turning his back on the situation he'd created once Kay was gone, unless…

Unless he really hadn't known about the baby. Unless the story Kay had told her was—unless it was—

"Ivy."

She looked up. Damian was standing over her; the helicopter had touched down. He reached for her seat belt. She ignored him, did it herself and walked to the door. Joe was already on the ground. He held up his arms and she let him help her down.

"Careful of the rotor wash," he yelled.

And then Damian's arm was around her waist and he led her to a long, black limousine.

"One for each city," Ivy said briskly. "How nice to be a potentate."

Damian looked at her as if she'd lost her mind. Perhaps she had, she thought, as the limo sped away.

That time in Athens, doing a spread for *In Vogue,* Ivy had spent hours, exhausting hours, in Kolonaki Square.

The photographer had shot her against the famous column that stood in the square. Against the well-dressed crowd. Against the charming cafés and shops. The stylist had dressed her in haute couture from Dolce & Gabbana and Armani and elegant boutiques in this upscale neighborhood.

Now, Damian took her into those same boutiques to buy her clothes.

"I don't need anything," she told him coldly.

"Of course you do. That's why I brought you here."

"I have my own things, thank you very much."

"Is that why your trousers don't close?"

She blushed, looked down and saw only the

slightly rounded contours of her gauzy shirt. Damian laughed softly.

"A good guess, *neh?*"

A clerk glided toward them. Damian took Ivy's hand and explained they needed garments that were loose-fitting. Ivy said nothing. This was his show; she'd be damned if she'd help. So he cleared his throat, let go of her hand and, instead, curved his arm around her and drew her close.

"My lady is pregnant."

There was an unmistakable ring of masculine pride in his voice. Ivy flashed him a cool look and wondered what would happen to all that macho arrogance if she added that she was pregnant, courtesy of a syringe.

"She carries my child," he said softly, and placed his hand over her rounded belly as if they were alone.

And that touch of his hand, not proprietary but tender, changed everything.

For the first time, Ivy let the picture she'd refused to envision fill her mind.

Damian, holding her in his arms. Undressing her. Carrying her to his bed, kissing her breasts, her belly. Parting her thighs, kneeling between them, his eyes dark with passion as he entered her and planted his seed in her womb.

"My child, *glyka mou,*" he whispered and this time, when he bent to her, Ivy rose on her toes, put her hand on the back of his head and brought his lips to hers.

The clerk in a tiny boutique on Voukourestiou Street said there was a little shop that specialized in maternity clothes only a few doors away.

Ivy said they didn't need anything else. A dozen

boxes and packages were already on their way by messenger to the limousine that waited on a quiet, shady street near the square.

To her amazement, Damian agreed.

"What we need is lunch." He smiled, tilted her face up to his and gave her a light kiss. "My son must be hungry by now."

Ivy laughed. "Using a baby as an excuse to fill your own belly is pathetic."

"But effective," he said, laughing with her.

They ate in a small café. The owner greeted Damian with a bear hug and the cook—his wife—hurried out from the kitchen, kissed Damian on both cheeks, kissed Ivy after introductions were made, then beamed and said something to Damian, who laughed and said *neh,* she was right.

"Right about what?" Ivy said, when they were alone.

Damian took her hand and brought it to his mouth. "She says you are carrying a strong, beautiful boy."

Ivy blushed. "Do I look that pregnant?"

His eyes darkened. "You look happy," he said softly. "Are you? Happy, today, with me?"

He had phrased the question carefully. She could answer it the same way. Or she could just say that she *was* happy, that when she didn't stop to think about why they were together, about how he'd come into her life, about what would happen next, she was incredibly happy. She was—she was—

"Lemonade," the café's owner said, setting two tall glasses in front of them. "For the proud papa—and the beautiful mama."

Ivy grabbed the glass as if it were a life preserver.

After a moment, Damian did, too.

* * *

She should have known Damian wouldn't leave without stopping at the maternity boutique.

They went there after lunch and found the jewel-like shop filled with exquisite, handmade clothes that could make even a woman whose belly was ballooning feel beautiful.

Desirable.

Ivy caught her breath. Damian heard her whisper of distress and brought her close against his side.

"Forgive me," he said softly. "I have exhausted you."

"No. I mean—I mean, I guess I am a little tired."

He smiled into her eyes. Pressed a kiss to her forehead.

"What is your favorite color, *glyka mou?*"

"My favorite color?"

"Green, to match your eyes? Gold, to suit your hair?" Instead of waiting for her answer, he turned to the hovering clerk. "We want everything you have in those colors."

"Damian!"

"Please, do not argue! You are tired. We are done shopping for the day."

His tone was imperious. Arrogant. Ivy knew she ought to tell him so...

Instead she buried her face against his shoulder and thought, *Just for today, just for now, let this all be a dream.*

Not the beautiful clothes, the elegant shops. They didn't matter.

Damian did.

She could pretend, couldn't she? Pretend he was her wonderful, incredible lover? Pretend they were together because they wanted to be? Pretend they had planned this baby, longed for it together?

What harm could it possibly do?

They flew home in the gathering twilight, trading the lights of the city for those of ships, of islands, of stars.

This time, Ivy went willingly into Damian's arms when he insisted on carrying her from the helicopter to the Jeep he'd left beside the airstrip hours before.

He put her into the passenger seat, then got behind the wheel and started the engine, let it idle as he stared out the windshield.

"Ivy. I have waited all day to tell you this." He cleared his throat. "I was very angry this morning."

Ivy sighed. So much for dreams. The day was over. Back to reality.

"I'm sure you were," she said quietly, "but—"

"Angry is too mild a word, *glyka mou*. I was furious."

"Damian. You have to understand that—"

"I have done a terrible thing."

"You *must* understand that…" She swung toward him. "What?"

"I brought you to my island so I could take care of you. Instead I've terrified you."

The soft night breeze tossed Ivy's hair over her cheek. She swept it back as she stared at the man seated beside her.

"I—I behaved badly that first night." He took a deep, deep breath, then expelled it. "And then, this morning… I had no right to turn my anger on you but I did and because of that, you walked a steep, long road under the hot sun."

Say something, Ivy told herself, for heaven's sake, say something!

"Walking is—walking is good for me."

"Ivy." His voice was rough. "I'm trying to apologize and—" He looked at her and smiled. "And it's not something I'm very good at."

Something in her softened. "Maybe because you don't do it very often," she said, smiling a little, too.

He grinned. "There are many people who would agree with you." He cleared his throat, engaged the gears and the Jeep moved forward. "So we will start over. I will take care of you."

"Damian. I don't need you to take care of me. I've been taking care of myself for a very long time."

"It's what I want."

Ivy hesitated. "Because of—because of the baby."

"That is part of it, of course. But I want—I want—"

He hesitated, too. What *did* he want? Things had seemed so clear this morning. He'd made Ivy his responsibility; that meant buying her whatever she needed.

But somewhere during the course of the day, that had changed. She'd gone from being his responsibility to being his pleasure and joy.

"I want to do the right thing," he said, hurrying the words because that was safer than trying to figure out where in hell this line of thought might lead. "I should have done that from the start instead of rushing off like a frustrated schoolboy the night I brought you here."

"You don't have to apologize," Ivy said quickly. This wasn't a topic she wanted to discuss. "I understood."

They had reached the palace. He pulled up in front of it, killed the engine and took her hands in his.

"I know it's no excuse but I've never lost control as

I did that night, *kardia mou*. I've never wanted a woman as I wanted you."

He spoke in the past tense. She understood that, too. He'd gone to Athens. Satisfied his—his needs.

"It was just as well that call came from my office. If I'd remained here, I don't know—I don't know what would have happened."

She stared at him. "You mean, you went to Athens on business?"

"What else would have taken me from you that night?" He gave a halfhearted laugh. "If anyone had ever suggested I would be grateful one of my tankers hit a reef…"

He hadn't left her for another woman's bed. Why did that mean so much?

"As for this child… No, don't look away from me." He cupped her chin and turned her face toward his. "How can we start over if we keep hiding things from each other? I did not know anything about a child. Do you really think, had I known, I would have abandoned it?"

Ivy shook her head. "Kay said—"

"Kay lied," he said sharply. "And that is the truth. I may not be a saint but I swear to you, I did not do these things. I did not ask Kay to become pregnant, and I certainly did not ask her to have a stranger become pregnant in her place."

"Me," Ivy said in a small, shaky voice.

"You," Damian said, bringing her hands to his lips. "But you are not a stranger any longer. You are a woman I know and admire."

"How can you admire me when you think—you think I did this for money? I didn't, Damian, I swear it. I didn't want to do it at all but—"

"But?"

But, I owed my stepsister more than I could ever repay.

She couldn't tell him that. The enormity of her debt. What would become of his admiration if she did? Only Kay knew her secret, and Kay had made her see that she must never tell anyone else.

"But," she whispered, "Kay took care of me after I—after I left foster care. I would have done anything to make her happy and so I said I'd do this…" Ivy bowed her head. "But I lied to myself. How could I have thought I'd be able to give up my—give up this baby?" Her voice broke. "Even the thought of it tears out my heart."

Damian took her in his arms, rocked her against him while she wept.

"Don't cry," he murmured. "You won't have to give up the baby, I promise." He pressed a kiss to her hair. "I am proud you carry my child, Ivy."

She looked up, eyes bright with tears. "Are you?"

"I only wish—I wish that I had put my seed deep in your womb as I made love to you." He kissed her; she clung to his shoulders as she kissed him back. "What I said in New York has not changed. I want to marry you."

"No. I know you want to do the right thing but—" She swallowed. "But I wouldn't be a good wife."

He smiled. "Have you been married before?" When she shook her head, his smile broadened. "Then, how can you know that?"

"I just do."

"We would start out together, *kardia mou,* I learning to be a good husband, you learning to be a good wife."

Ivy shook her head. "It would never work."

"Of course it would." Impatience roughened his voice. "Look at what we already have in common. A child we both love." His hands tightened on her shoulders. "I want my son," he said bluntly. "And I intend to have him. You can become my wife and his mother—or I'll take him from you. I don't want to hurt you but if I must, I will."

He was right, never mind all her pie-in-the-sky scheming this morning. Damian would win in a custody battle, even if she told the court her secret. He was the prince of a respected royal house. She was nobody.

Worse than nobody.

"What will it be? A courtroom? Or marriage?"

Ivy bowed her head, took a steadying breath, then looked up and met Damian's eyes.

"I can't marry you, Damian, even if—even if I wanted to. The thing is—the thing is—"

"For God's sake, what?"

"I don't like…" Her voice fell to a shaky whisper. "I don't like sex."

She didn't know what reaction she'd expected. Laughter? Anger? Disbelief? Surely not his sudden stillness. The muscle, knotting in his jaw. The way he looked at her, as if he were seeing her for the first time.

"You don't like—"

"No."

"Is that why you stopped me the other night?"

Ivy nodded. She would never tell him everything but he was entitled, at least, to know this.

He nodded, too. Then he got out of the Jeep, opened her door, drew her gently to her feet and into his arms.

"It's late," he said gruffly. "Much too late an hour of

the night for truths and secrets like this. I'm going to take you to your room and put you to bed."

He believed her. She was stunned. Men who came on to her, who called her frigid when she turned them away, never did.

He lifted her into his arms and she let him do it, loving the strength of his embrace, the warmth of his body, wishing with all her heart that things were different. That she was different.

And realized, too late, that the door he shouldered open, the bed he brought her to, was not hers.

It was his.

She began to protest. He silenced her with a kiss that left her breathless.

CHAPTER NINE

MOONLIGHT washed through the French doors and lit Ivy in its creamy spill.

Damian wanted to see her face but when he tried to lift her chin, she shook her head.

Was it true? Did this stunning, sensual woman dislike sex?

Earlier in the day, sitting on a too-small sofa in one of the boutiques, trying not to look as conspicuous as he felt, trying, as well, to figure out how in hell he'd gotten himself into this because he'd never, not once in his life, gone shopping with a woman—sitting there, arms folded, while Ivy changed into a dress in the fitting room, the salesclerk had bent down and whispered how flattered the shop was to have Ivy Madison as a customer.

Damian had frowned. How did the clerk know Ivy? Then he'd happened to glance at a glossy magazine on a table beside him and there was Ivy, smiling seductively from the cover.

In the days since she'd walked into his life, he'd thought of her as a lot of different things, all the way from scam artist to mother of his child. And, yes, gorgeous, too.

What man wouldn't notice that?

But he'd never thought of her as a woman whose face was known around the world.

He'd picked up the magazine, opened to a spread of Ivy modeling beachwear. She stood facing the camera in a white halter gown that clung to her body. In a crimson bikini that paid homage to her breasts and long legs. In a butter-yellow robe that hung open just enough to make his pulse accelerate.

He thought of other men, faceless strangers looking at those same photos, feeling what he felt, and he wanted to hunt the bastards down and make sure they understood they were wasting their time dreaming about her because she belonged solely to him.

Crazy, he'd told himself.

And then Ivy, his Ivy, had walked out of the dressing room, stepped onto a little platform in a gown he supposed was attractive—except, he hadn't really noticed.

All he'd noticed was her.

She was beautiful. Not in the way she was in the magazine, gazing in sultry splendor at the camera but as she was right then, a flesh and blood woman looking questioningly at him.

"What do you think?" she'd said.

What he'd thought was that she was so beautiful she stole his breath away.

"Very nice," he'd said.

The understatement of the year, but how did you tell a woman you were a heartbeat away from taking her in your arms, carrying her into the dressing room, kicking the damned door closed and making love to her? Doing it again and again until she was trembling with passion, until she admitted that she wanted him, that she would always want him.

Now she'd told him she didn't like sex.

It could be another bit of deceit to tempt him further into her web.

Damian's jaw tightened.

It could be...but it wasn't. He remembered what had happened in this same room, three nights ago. How she'd responded to him with dizzying abandon until he'd tried to take things further.

Without question, she'd told him the truth.

"Ivy?"

She didn't answer. He brushed the knuckles of his hand lightly against her cheek.

"Is that what happened the other night? Is that the reason you stopped me?"

"Yes."

The word was a sigh. He had to bend his head to hear it.

"You should have told me," he said softly.

"Tell you something like that?" She gave a forlorn little laugh. "When a man's about to—about to—to try to—" A deep breath. "I don't want to talk about it. I just thought you should know why I could never—I mean, the idea of marriage is out of the question anyway but—but if—if there were even the most remote possibility—"

"You're wrong, *agapi mou*. About everything."

His voice was so sure. God, he was so arrogant! And yet, right now, that arrogance made her smile. Despite herself, Ivy turned and lifted her eyes to his.

"Doesn't it ever occur to you," she said softly, "that there are times it's you who's wrong?"

"But you see, sweetheart, I wasn't going to have sex with you. I was going to make love to you."

"It's the same—"

He kissed her. Kissed her without demanding anything but her compliance, his mouth warm and tender against hers. Kissed her until he felt her tremble, though not with fear.

"You don't like sex," he said softly. "But you like my kisses."

"Damian. I can't. Really, I just—"

He kissed her again, just as gently, and felt a fierce rush of pleasure when her mouth softened under his.

"Damian." Her voice shook. "I don't think—"

"Shh." His hands spread across her back, applying just a little pressure when he kissed her again, enough to part her lips and touch the tip of her tongue with his.

A whisper of sound rose in her throat. Did she move closer or did he? It took all his self-control not to pull her into his arms.

"Sex is a physical act, *glyka mou*. It's part of making love but it's hardly all of it."

"I don't see—"

"No. You don't. Let me show you, then. Just another kiss," he added, when she began to shake her head. "I only want to taste you. Will you permit me to do that?"

He didn't wait for her answer. Instead he put his mouth against hers.

"Open to me," he said thickly. A second slipped by. Then she moaned, rose on her toes, tipped her head back and let him take the kiss deeper.

Damian kissed her over and over, his tongue in her mouth, his hands buried in the chestnut and gold spill of her hair.

He told himself he would keep his promise. That he would only taste her. But as her skin heated, as she sighed with pleasure, he put his lips against her throat, slipped her blouse from her shoulders, kissed his way to the vee of her silk T-shirt.

"Ivy," he whispered, his hands spreading over her midriff, the tips of his fingers brushing the undersides of her breasts. "Ivy, *kardia mou…*"

Her hands lifted, knotted in his shirt. His name sighed from her lips.

The room began to blur.

He told himself to go slowly. To do no more than he'd said he would. But she was leaning into him now, her hands were cool on his nape and he bent his head to her breasts, kissed them through the silky fabric of her shirt.

She made a broken little sound deep in her throat and arched her back. The simple motion made an offering of her beaded nipples, taut and visible beneath her T-shirt.

It would have taken a saint to refuse such a gift.

Damian was no saint.

He kissed the delicate beads of silk-covered flesh. Drew them into his mouth, first one and then the other. Ivy's cries grew sharper. Hungrier.

So did his need.

He dropped to his knees. Lifted her shirt and found he'd been right about the half-closed zipper.

Slowly he eased the trousers down her hips and legs.

"Damian," she said unsteadily.

He looked up at her. "I'm just going to undress you," he whispered. "Then I'll put you to bed and if you want me to leave, I will. I promise."

She hesitated. Then she stepped out of the trousers and when he saw her like that, wearing the silk T-shirt, her long legs bare, her feet encased in foolishly high heels, he wondered why in hell he'd made such a promise.

But he would keep it.

He would keep it by stopping now. By standing up. By—all right, by reaching under the T, undoing her bra, only because she wouldn't want to sleep with it on…

Ivy stumbled back. "Don't! Please, don't."

Her voice was high; her eyes were wide with fear and, in a heartbeat, Damian understood.

She'd said she didn't like sex. He'd foolishly, arrogantly assumed she was simply a woman unawakened.

He knew better now.

Ivy, his Ivy, didn't like sex because she was terrified of it. A man had hurt her. Taught her that sex was painful or evil or ugly.

Damian spat out a sharp, four-letter word. Ivy began to weep.

"I told you," she sobbed, "I told you how it would be—"

"Who did this to you?"

She didn't answer. He cursed again, took her in his arms, ignored her attempts to free herself and wrapped her in his embrace.

"Ivy. *Agapi mou. Kardia mou.* Do not cry. Ivy, my Ivy…"

He'd lost his accent his second year at Yale but it was back now, roughening his words and then he was talking in Greek, not the modern language he'd grown up speaking but the ancient one he'd studied in prep school.

The Greek of the Spartans and Athenians. His warrior ancestors.

He knew what they would have done. It was what he longed to do. Find the man who'd done this to Ivy and kill him.

Her soft, desperate sobs broke his heart.

He held her against him, rocking her, whispering to her, soft, sweet words he had never said to a woman before, never wanted to say and, at last, her tears stopped.

Gently he scooped her into his arms and put her in the center of his bed, stroked her tousled hair back from her damp cheeks.

"It's all right," he murmured. "It's all right, sweetheart. Go to sleep, *agapimeni*. I'll stay here and keep you safe."

He drew the comforter over her. She clutched at it and rolled onto her side, turning her back to him. He wanted to reach for her again, to lie down and hold her, but instinct warned him not to. She was too fragile right now; God only knew what might push her over the edge.

So he sat beside her, watching until her breathing slowed and her lashes drooped against her cheeks.

"Ivy?" he said softly.

She was asleep.

Damian dropped a light kiss on her hair. Then he went into his dressing room, took off his clothes and put on an old, soft pair of Yale sweats. He padded back into the bedroom, drew an armchair next to the bed, sat down, stretched out his long legs and considered all the creative ways a man could deal with a son of a bitch who'd taught his Ivy that sex, the most intimate act a man and woman could share, was a thing to be feared.

He'd go from A to Z, he thought grimly. But "Assault" was too general. "Beating" was too simple.

"Castration" was a lot better. He stayed with that scenario until sleep finally dragged him under.

Something woke him.

The moon had disappeared, chased into hiding by wind and rain. The room was as black and frigid as Hecate's heart.

Damian padded quickly to the French doors and closed them. Damn, it was cold! Was Ivy warm enough under the comforter? It was too dark to see anything but the outline of the big bed.

He turned on a lamp, adjusting the switch until the light was only a soft glow. Ivy lay as he'd left her but the covers had dropped from her shoulder.

He shut off the light. Carefully leaned over the bed, began drawing up the comforter...

Zzzzt!

A streak of blinding light, then the roar of thunder rolling across the sea.

Ivy sprang up in bed, saw him leaning over her... and screamed.

"Ivy! Sweetheart. Don't be afraid. It's me. It's only me."

He caught her in his arms, ignored the jab that caught him in the eye and held her against him, stroking her, whispering to her. An eternity seemed to pass until, finally, she shuddered and went still.

"Damian?"

Her voice was thready. He drew her even closer, willing his strength into her.

"Yes, *agapimeni*. It's me."

Another shudder went through her. "I thought—I thought—"

He could only imagine what she'd thought. Rage, deep and ugly as a flood tide, filled him, left him struggling to keep his composure.

"You thought it was old Hephaestus, playing games with lightning bolts on Mount Olympus," he said with forced cheerfulness.

Was that tiny sound a laugh?

"Storms here can be pretty fierce during the summer. They scared the heck out of me when I was little, and it didn't help that my nanny would glare at me and say, 'You see, Your Highness? That's what happens when little boys don't listen to their nannies.'"

He'd dropped his voice to a husky growl that was less his long-ago nanny's and more a really bad Count Dracula, but it worked. His Ivy laughed. A definite laugh, this time, one that made him offer a silent word of thanks just in case old Hephaestus happened to be within earshot.

"That wasn't very nice of her."

"No, but it was effective. For the next few days, I'd be the model of princely decorum."

"And then?"

Lightning, followed by the crash of thunder, rolled across the sky again. Ivy trembled and Damian tightened his arms around her. "And then," he said, "I'd revert to the catch-me-if-you-can little devil I actually was." His smile faded. "You'll be fine, *glyka mou*. I won't let anything happen to you, I promise."

She leaned back in his embrace and looked up at him, her face a pale, lovely oval.

"Thank you," she whispered.

"For what?"

"For—" She hesitated. "For being so—so... For being so nice."

Nice? He'd bullied her, berated her, accused her of being a cheat and a liar. He'd forced her to come with him to Greece, told her he owned her...

"I haven't been nice," he said brusquely. "I've been impatient and arrogant. It is I who should thank you for tolerating me."

That rated a smile. "We're even, then. I'll forgive you and you'll forgive me."

He smiled back at her. A moment slipped by and his smile faded. "Ivy? Are you all right?"

"I'm fine."

"Good." God, how he wanted to kiss her. Just one kiss to tell her he would keep her safe from lightning and thunder and, most of all, safe from whatever terrible thing had once happened to her. "Good," he said briskly, and cleared his throat. "So. Let me tuck you in and—"

"Where are you sleeping? If I'm taking up your bed—"

"Don't worry about me."

"But where..."

"Right in that chair. I, ah, I thought it would be a good idea to be here in case, you know, in case you needed me."

"You? In that little chair? Where do you put your legs?"

He grinned. "They say a little suffering is good for the soul."

"It looks like a lot of suffering to me."

"Easy," he said lightly. "First you tell me I'm nice. Then you say I'm a candidate for sainthood. If you aren't careful—"

"Sleep with me."

Her voice was low, the words rushed. He told himself he'd misunderstood her but he hadn't, otherwise why would a pink stain be creeping into her cheeks?

"Just—just share the bed with me, Damian. Nothing else. I just—I don't want to think of you, all cramped up in that chair." She licked her lips. "If you won't share it, I'll have to sleep in the guest room. Alone. And—and I really don't want to. Be alone, I mean. Unless—unless you don't want—"

"Move over," he said, his voice gruff, his heart racing.

Ivy scooted away. He climbed onto the bed, slid under the covers, held his breath and then thought, to hell with it, and he put his arm around her waist and drew her into the curve of his body.

"Good night, *agapi mou*," he murmured.

"Good night, Damian."

He closed his eyes. Time passed. The storm moved off. Ivy lay unmoving in his embrace, so still that she had to be asleep and he—he was going to lose his mind. He *would* be a candidate for sainthood, by morning.

"Damian?"

He swallowed hard. "Yes, sweetheart?"

Slowly she turned toward him. He could feel her breath on his face.

Her hand touched his stubbled jaw; her fingers drifted like feathers over his mouth.

"Ivy…"

Her hand cupped the back of his head and she brought his lips down to hers.

His heart turned over.

"Ivy," he whispered again but she shook her head, kissed him and drew even closer.

One of them had to be dreaming.

Her lips parted. The tip of her tongue touched the seam of his mouth. He wanted to roll her on her back, open her mouth to his, savage her mouth with kisses.

But he wouldn't.

He wouldn't.

He would do only what she asked of him. He was not a saint but neither was he a beast.

Ivy whispered his name. Lay her thigh over his.

Damian groaned, caught her hands and held them against his chest.

"Sweetheart," he said raggedly, "*glyka mou*. I can't—" He cleared his throat. "Let's—let's sit up. In the chair. I'll hold you and—and when sunrise comes, we can watch it together and—and—"

She silenced him with a kiss that told him everything a man could hope to hear. Still, he held back and she took the initiative, rolling onto her back, holding him close, arching her body against his.

"Ivy," he whispered, and let himself tumble into the hot abyss with her.

He kissed her mouth. Her eyes. Her throat. She gave soft little cries of pleasure and each cry filled his soul.

He kissed her breasts through the thin silk T-shirt, sucked her nipples into his mouth and she went crazy beneath him, sobbing his name, clutching his shoulders, and he thought, *Slow down, slow down, God, slow down or this will end much too fast.*

But he was lost.

Lost in Ivy's scent, in her taste, in the silk of her hair and the heat of her skin.

He pushed up her shirt. Bared her breasts. Kissed the creamy slopes, teased the pale pink nipples, her sweet cries urging him on.

He sat her up. Pulled the shirt over her head. Unhooked her bra and her breasts, like the most precious fruit, tumbled into his hands.

He kissed them, kissed her belly, round and taut with his child and thought, as he had before, how perfect it would be if he and she had made this child together.

Then he stopped thinking because she was tugging at his sweatshirt.

He reared back and tugged it off. She arched against him, her breasts hot against his chest, and her moans of ecstasy almost unmanned him.

Her panties were the merest whisper of silk. He drew them down her legs and she arched again so that he sank into the spread of her thighs.

"Ivy," he said thickly.

"Yes," she whispered. "Please, yes."

She lifted her face and he kissed her, tasting her tears, tasting her sweetness, and something stirred deep, deep inside him, something stirred within his heart.

And then he was inside her. Inside her and she was so tight. So tight…

"Damian," she sighed, and put her hand between them.

The world spun away.

He groaned, thrust forward and Ivy cried out and came apart in his arms.

He held on as long as he could. Sheathing himself within her. Pulling back until it was torture, then sinking deep, feeling her come again and again until, finally, he let himself go with her. Fly into the night, into the sky, into the universe.

And knew, as he collapsed against her, that sex was, indeed, only sex. Making love was what really mattered.

And though he'd been with many women, he had never really made love until tonight.

CHAPTER TEN

DAMIAN was asleep.

Ivy had slept, too. For a little while, anyway, safe and warm in his embrace.

Then she'd awakened.

And, just that quickly, the memories came rushing back.

She'd lain beside him for another few minutes, telling herself not to let this happen. Not to spoil the wonder of Damian's lovemaking with the ugliness of those memories.

It hadn't worked.

Finally, carefully, she'd slipped from under the curve of her lover's arm and risen from the bed.

A soft cashmere throw lay at its foot. She'd wrapped herself in it, held her breath while she opened the French doors and stepped out on the terrace.

When would she finally be able to forget?

A little while ago, when the fury of the storm had invaded her dreams, it spun her back in time to another night a long, long time ago.

No, she'd whimpered, deep in the dream, *no!*

It hadn't mattered.

She'd come awake in terror. And when she saw the figure bending over her, that terror had wrapped its bony hands around her throat.

"No," she'd screamed—and then Damian had spoken her name.

He was the man leaning over her bed, not a fat monster who stunk of beer and sweat.

He hadn't grabbed her breast, squeezed it, laughed as he ripped her nightgown open.

He hadn't clamped a sweaty palm over her mouth as she tried to fight him off, her fifteen-year-old self no match for a man who earned his living swinging a pick ax.

Not a sound, he'd said, his stinking breath washing over her. *You make one noise, just one, I'll tell the social worker you stole money outta my wallet and you'll be back in Juvie Placement so fast it'll make your head spin.*

She hadn't stolen anything. Ever. The first time, in a different foster home, they'd said she'd taken a hundred dollars. She hadn't—but Kay said she had to be lying because the only other person who could have done it was her. Kay. Was Ivy accusing her of theft?

Kay stayed in that home. Ivy was sent back to the Placement facility. Eventually they'd put her in another foster home.

Kay turned eighteen and left the system.

"See you," she said.

And Ivy was alone.

Six months in one place. Three in another. Bad places. Dirty places. And then, finally, a place where the woman just looked right through her and the man smiled and said, *Call me Daddy.*

Ivy had felt her heart lift.

Daddy, she'd said, and even though he wasn't like her real daddy—whom she barely remembered—or her stepfather, Kay's father, whom she'd loved with all her heart—even though he wasn't, he was nice.

At least, that was what she thought.

He bought her a doll. Some books. And when he began coming into her room at night, to tuck her in, she'd felt a little funny because he also took to kissing her on the cheek but if he was her daddy, her real daddy, that was okay, wasn't it?

A light wind blowing in over the sea raised goose bumps on her skin. Ivy shuddered and drew the cashmere blanket more closely around her.

And then it all changed. One night, a storm was roaring outside. Lightning. Thunder. Rain. It scared her but she finally fell asleep—and woke to see the man she called Daddy standing over her bed.

Even now, all these years later, the memory was sheer agony.

He'd hurt her. Hurt her bad. He came to her each night, night after night, and when she finally tried to tell the woman, she'd slapped her in the face, called her a slut...

And Kay had come.

Ivy had flown to embrace her but Kay had pushed her away.

"What'd you do, huh?" she'd said coldly. "Don't give me that innocent look. Did you play games with this man like you did with my father?"

"What games?" Ivy had said in bewilderment. "I loved your father. He treated me as if I were his own daughter."

The look on her stepsister's face had been as frigid as her voice. "Only one problem, Little Miss Innocent. He already had a daughter. Me."

She'd lived with Kay for a few months but she knew she was in the way. And then, a couple of weeks after she turned seventeen, a man walked up to her on Madison Avenue, handed her his card and said, "Give me a call and we'll see if you have what it takes to become a model."

Kay had said yes, fine, do whatever you want. Just remember, never tell anybody what you did because they'll tell you how disgusting you really are.

Ivy moved out, the agency sent her to Milan, moved her into an apartment with five other girls. She sent Kay cards and letters that all went unanswered until she made the cover of *Glamour Girl* and Kay called to say she was so sorry they'd lost touch and how proud she was to be her sister…

"Glyka mou?"

Ivy spun around as Damian walked out onto the balcony. He'd pulled on his sweatpants. They hung low on his hips, accentuating his naked chest, muscled shoulders and arms, the abs most male models worked like machines to develop.

Beautiful. He was so beautiful. And so good and decent and kind…

"Sweetheart." He gathered her into his arms. "What's the matter?"

She shook her head, not trusting herself to speak, afraid that if she did, the lump that had suddenly risen in her throat would give way and she'd burst into tears of joy.

"Agapimeni." He tilted her face to his and brushed his lips gently over hers. "Tell me what's happened. Why did you leave me?"

I'll never leave you, she thought. *Never, not as long as you want me!*

"I just—" She swallowed, blinked away the silly burn of tears. "I woke up and—and I could still hear the storm, way off in the distance, and I wanted to—I wanted to see…"

Smiling, he cupped her face and threaded his fingers into her hair.

"A little while ago, you were afraid of the storm."

"That was before you made me see I had nothing to be afraid of."

Something dark flickered in his eyes. "Never," he said fiercely. "Not as long as I'm here to protect you."

Her heart lifted. How wrong she'd been about this man. Arrogant? Overpowering? Never. He was simply sure of himself, and strong.

And tender. And caring. And she felt—she felt—

"It was more than the storm you feared." His arms tightened around her. "Do you want to tell me about it?"

Yes. God yes, she did! But not yet. Not now. Not when her feelings were so new, so confused.

"It's all right." He kissed her. "You don't have to tell me anything you don't want to tell me."

"It isn't that. It's just…" She hesitated. "What's happened. This. It's all so—so new…"

"You mean, us," he said. When she nodded, he lifted her in his arms and carried her through the French doors. Gently he lay her on the bed and came down beside her.

"Are you happy?"

She smiled. "I'm very happy."

Slowly he eased the cashmere blanket from her shoulders, revealing her breasts, her belly, her body to his eyes.

"You're the most beautiful woman in the world," he whispered. "And I'm the luckiest man."

He dipped his head. Kissed her throat. Bent lower and circled a nipple with the tip of his tongue.

Ivy trembled. "Oh. Oh God, that feels—it feels—"

He licked the nipple. Sucked it into his mouth. She wound her arms around his neck, stunned at the sudden sharp longing low in her belly.

"How does it feel?" he said gruffly. "Tell me."

"Wonderful. Damian. It feels—"

His hand slipped down her belly, into the curls between her thighs, into the heat between her thighs, and found her clitoris.

Ivy moaned with pleasure and arched against his fingers.

"Please," she whispered. "Please."

"Please, what?" he said, and the thickness in his voice added to her excitement.

"Please," she sighed, "make love to me again."

He kissed her mouth. Kissed her belly. Parted her thighs and put his mouth to her and the first touch of his tongue sent her flying.

And then he was inside her, deep inside her, and she was lost. He said her name and she disintegrated into a million, billion pieces that flew to the far ends of the universe…

And knew the truth.

She had fallen in love with the complicated, impossible, wonderful man in her arms.

She lay beneath him, arms wrapped around him, his weight bearing her down into the mattress, his heart racing against hers, his skin damp from their lovemaking.

Until this moment even thinking about those things—a man's body on hers, the thud of his heart, the scent of his sweat… Just imagining those things, remembering them, was enough to bring a dizzying wave of nausea.

But this was Damian.

And this was, as he'd promised, the difference between having sex and making love.

I love you, she thought, *Damian, I love you…*

Had she said the words? Was that why he was rolling away?

"Don't go," she said, before she could stop herself.

Damian's arms closed around her. He drew her close to him, their faces inches apart.

"I'm not going anywhere, *glyka mou,*" he whispered. "I'm just too heavy to lie on top of you."

"You're not."

He kissed her, his lips warm against hers.

"My sweet fraud," he said softly.

It was a soft, teasing endearment. She knew that. Still, it hurt because she *was* a fraud.

She hadn't told him about her past.

Hadn't told him about his baby.

And she had to tell him. He had to know. But when? When?

"You're trembling." Damian drew the comforter over them both. "Better?"

"Yes. Fine."

"Mmm." He grinned. "Indeed you were." He gave her a long, tender kiss. "I was afraid I might hurt you, sweetheart. You were so tight."

His voice was low and filled with concern. This was either the exact moment to tell him everything—or the exact moment not to.

How could she admit to her ugly past?

How could she admit to the lie she'd told him?

"Sweetheart? Did I hurt you? God, if I did…"

"No! Oh, no, Damian, you didn't hurt me." Ivy took his hand, brought it to her mouth and kissed it. "What we did—"

"Making love."

"Yes. It was wonderful."

He held her against him for a long moment. Then he cupped her face and tilted it to his.

"I'm sorry I frightened you before."

"It wasn't your fault. I was—I was dreaming. And then I heard the thunder and I saw the lightning and—"

"And, you thought I was someone else. Someone who'd hurt you."

She couldn't lie, not when his arms were around her. "Yes."

Rage swept over him. Her whisper only confirmed what he'd already suspected.

"A man."

Ivy buried her face against his throat.

"Who?"

She shook her head. "I don't want to talk about it."

Yes, but he did. He wanted a name. He wanted to find this faceless son of a bitch and kill him.

Ah, God, Ivy was trembling and he knew damned well it had nothing to do with the temperature of the room. Damian cursed himself for being an ass.

"Forgive me, sweetheart." He kissed her hair, her temple, her mouth. "I'm a fool to talk about these things at a time like this."

"You're not a fool," she said fiercely, looking into his eyes. "You're a good, kind, wonderful man."

He forced a smile to his face. "That's quite an improvement over being—let's see. An SOB, an arrogant bastard, a son of—"

She laughed, as he'd hoped she would. "Well, sometimes… No. Seriously you're not any of those things I called you."

His hand moved slowly down her spine, cupped her bottom, drew her more closely against him.

"We didn't know each other," he said softly. "And it's my fault. I stormed into your life—"

"Seems to me I was the one who did the storming."

Good. She was smiling. He hadn't spoiled this amazing night for her after all.

No more questions…for now. But he would ask them again. A monster had done something terrible to Ivy.

Something sexual. Something violent.

Had he been caught? Had he paid for what he'd done? Not that it mattered. He would find the man and deal with him in his own way…

"Damian?"

He blinked. "Yes?"

"I'm glad we stormed into each other's lives."

He smiled and lifted her face to his so he could kiss her again. How had he lived his life without this woman?

"So am I. And now we have all the time in the world to get to know each other."

Ivy put her hand against his jaw. "Being with you tonight has been—has been—"

"Making love, you mean."

Her heart lifted. "Making love with you, yes. It was—it was so wonderful…"

How he loved the sound of her voice. The feel of her in his arms. How he loved—how he loved—

"For me, too," he said huskily. "I've never—I mean, you and I…" He cleared his throat, amazed at how difficult it was to say the next words but then, they were a kind of commitment, given all the women in his past. "What happened between us is… It was very special, *glyka mou*. I've never experienced anything like it before."

Ivy's face was solemn. "I'm glad because…" She touched the tip of her tongue to her lips. "Because this was—this is—it's the very first time I ever—I ever—"

She was blushing. Amazing, that this beautiful, sophisticated woman would blush when she talked about having an orgasm.

Amazing, too, that his damnable ego took pleasure in the thought that he had done for her what no other lover had done.

"Your first orgasm," he said softly, and smiled. "Part of me is sorry that's been denied you but I have to admit, part of me is… What?"

"I'm not talking about having an orgasm." Her voice was so soft he had to strain to hear it. "I'm talking about…" She swallowed. "You're right," she said, rushing the words together. "Something did happen to me, a long time ago. And because it did, I never took a lover until—until—"

The hurried words trailed off. Ivy tried to look away but Damian wouldn't let her. He cupped her face, kissed her mouth, told her what honor she had brought him, by letting him be her first lover.

Then he rolled her gently on her back.

"And your only lover, for the rest of our lives."

He kissed her. Caressed her. Touched her as if she were as fragile as a cobweb until she sobbed his name and showed him with her mouth, her hands, her body that she would not break…

Showed him, without words, what was in her heart.

Showed him that she had fallen deeply, forever in love.

They flew to Athens the next morning to see an obstetrician, who examined Ivy, looked over the records that Damian, ever in command, had somehow had transferred from her New York OB-GYN, smiled and said, *neh,* everything was fine.

Was she certain? asked Damian.

The doctor said she was.

Because, Damian said, he'd noticed things.

The doctor and Ivy both looked at him. "What things?" they said in unison.

Well, his Ivy didn't eat as much as she should.

His Ivy? The phrase went straight to Ivy's heart. She smiled and put her hand in his.

"My appetite's just fine."

"Yes, *glyka mou,* but you are eating for two."

"Ms. Madison's weight is right on target."

Damian didn't look convinced but had another question. What about exercise? He had walked her all around Kolonaki Square only yesterday. Was it too much? Should he have permitted—

"Permitted?" Ivy said, her eyebrows rising again.

Should he have let her do that? Damian asked

"Ms. Madison is in excellent health, Your Highness. And," the doctor added gently, "she is hardly the first woman to have a baby."

Damian's authoritative air vanished. "I know that," he said, "but I am the first man to have one." A beat of silence; the doctor smiled but not Ivy. "I mean, I mean—"

"You mean this is your first child," the doctor said. "Of course, Your Highness. And I promise you, everything is fine."

Outside, on the street, Ivy turned to Damian. "I understand why you're so concerned. You—you lost a baby, with my sister."

"I *thought* I lost a baby," Damian said carefully. "But it was a lie."

"Yes." Her eyes clouded. "A terrible lie. But believing you'd really lost a baby must have been almost as bad as having it happen."

Damian wanted to take her in his arms and kiss her, but they were on a crowded street. He made do with taking her hand, bringing it to his lips and pressing a kiss into the palm.

"I'm concerned because of you," he said. "If anything happened to you…" He took a deep breath. "Ivy. You are—you are—"

My love.

The words were right there, on the tip of his tongue, but that was crazy. He hardly knew this woman. And there were still so many unanswered questions…

Besides, a man didn't fall in love after, what, a week? There was no reason to be impulsive. To make a move he might regret.

"You are important to me." He brought her hand to his mouth, kissed the palm and folded her fingers over the kiss. "Very important."

Ivy nodded. They weren't the words she yearned to hear, but they were close.

"I'm glad, because—because you're very important to me, too."

A smile lit his face. "Words meant to feed a man's ego," he said teasingly.

"Words that are true. Being with you, carrying your baby…" She hesitated, afraid she would blurt out too much. "I've never been this happy. And I want you to know that—that no matter what happens, you will always be—you will always be—"

She fell silent as their eyes met.

Damian's heart turned over at what he saw in her face.

Years ago, he, Lucas and Nicolo had celebrated surviving finals week at Yale by driving to an airport in a little town called Danielson.

They'd taken a couple of hours of instruction, strapped on parachutes and boarded a plane after drawing slips of paper to decide which of them would go first.

He'd won.

"Or lost," Nicolo had said, grinning.

It came back to him now, the way he'd felt standing in the plane's open door, the wind trying to pluck him out, the ground beckoning from a million miles below.

What in hell am I doing? he'd thought.

"Jump," his instructor had yelled.

And he had.

God, it had been incredible. Stepping into space. Soaring above the earth, then falling toward it.

Incredible.

He'd jumped for years after that but as much as he'd loved skydiving, he'd never quite felt the excitement, the sheer wonder of that first time.

Until now.

Until he saw the smile in Ivy's eyes. Felt his heart thump as she lay her palms against his chest.

He reminded himself that he really knew nothing about her.

Reminded himself that she hadn't given a reasonable answer as to why she'd agreed to Kay's incredible request.

And now there were more questions. Who had hurt her? Why wouldn't she talk about it?

One call to a private investigator and he'd have the answers he needed in, what, a week?

That was what he had to do. He was a logical man. He always had been. That was how he'd saved Aristedes Shipping. With logic. Common sense. By taking one step at a time.

By *not* jumping into space.

Skydiving, skiing down a glacier… A man could run risks in such things but not in those that were life-changing.

Damian took Ivy's hands in his. They were icy-cold, despite the heat of the day. She had opened her heart to him and now she was waiting for him to say something.

And he would.

Something logical. Something sensible. Something that would not put him at risk…

"Ivy," he said, "my beautiful Ivy. I love you. I adore you. Will you be my wife?"

She stared at him as if he'd lost his mind. Well, maybe he had. But when she smiled, and her eyes filled with tears, and she said she loved him with all her heart and yes, she would be his wife, yes, yes, yes…

It wasn't anything like that first jump.

It was ten thousand times better.

CHAPTER ELEVEN

Ivy stood ankle-deep in the surf, her face turned up to the hot kiss of the sun.

A month ago, Minos had been a forbidding chunk of rock rearing up from a depressingly dark sea.

Now, it was paradise.

White sand beaches. Towering volcanic rock. Firs, pines, poplars that climbed its slopes, anemones and violets that poked slyly from the deep green grass.

And around it all, the Aegean, wine-dark and magnificent, just as the poet, Homer, had described it centuries before.

Could a place look so different just because you were happy?

Yes. Oh, yes, it could.

Not just a place. The world. The universe. And happy wasn't the right word to describe how she felt.

She was—she was complete.

Being with Damian, being part of his life, having him a part of hers, was wonderful.

He was everything. The sun, the moon, the stars... She laughed out loud, threw up her arms and did a little dance right there, as the wavelets foamed around her ankles.

Surely nobody had ever been this much in love. It just wasn't possible.

Ivy eased down to the sand, legs outstretched in the warm surf, arms back, basking in the glorious warmth of the Greek sun.

The only thing warmer was Damian's love.

That so much joy had come from something that had started so badly... Not the baby, she thought quickly, putting a protective hand over her belly. Never that. She'd wanted the baby almost the moment she'd missed her first period and known, for sure, she was pregnant.

Known she wanted the baby—and that she'd made a terrible mistake, agreeing to Kay's awful plan.

That was the bad start. The plan. Not the original one, which had been hard enough to say "yes" to, but the one Kay had dropped on her at the last possible second.

How could she have agreed to it?

Ivy shut her eyes. The truth was, she'd never agreed to it in her heart.

The joy of the sunny morning fell away.

In the end, Kay had asked too much of her. She'd owed her so much, yes, so much, but giving up the baby?

She knew now that she could not, would not have done it.

Wasn't it time to explain that, to explain everything, to Damian?

Slowly Ivy rose to her feet, tucked her hands into the back pockets of her white shorts and began walking along the sand.

Of course it was.

At the beginning, Damian had assumed she'd made

a devil's bargain. He knew better, now, that she'd never do something like this for money.

And because he loved her, he'd stopped asking.

That didn't mean he wasn't entitled to the truth.

It was just that telling him meant telling him everything, starting with what had occurred when she was fifteen and ending with the day a doctor was to implant Kay's eggs, mixed with Damian's sperm, in her womb.

Except—except, it hadn't happened that way.

Ivy swung blindly toward the sea, remembering her stepsister's face that day.

Kay had shown up at Ivy's apartment hours ahead of their scheduled appointment at the fertility clinic.

"Everything's changed," she'd said desperately. "My doctor says my eggs are no good. There's no point in implanting them inside you."

Ivy had taken Kay in her arms, patted her back, said she was sorry even as a mean little voice inside her whispered *You know you're not really sorry, you're relieved. Carrying a baby, even one that wasn't actually yours, would have been agony to give up.*

"Oh, Ivy," Kay had sobbed, "what am I going to do? You have to help me!"

"I wish I could but—"

Kay had raised her face. Amazingly her tears had not spoiled her makeup.

"Do you?" she'd said. "Do you really wish you could help me?"

And she'd laid out a plan so detailed, so complete, only a fool—a fool like Ivy—would have believed she'd just come up with it.

Ivy had listened. Halfway through, she'd raised her hands in horror.

"No! Kay, I can't do that! You can't really ask me to—"

Kay's eyes had darkened. "So much for all these years you've told me how grateful you were I took you out of that foster home."

"Of course I'm grateful! But—"

"Out of a situation you'd created."

"I didn't. I didn't!"

"Of course you did," Kay had said coldly. "Flirting with that man. Hanging all over him."

"I never did! I was just a kid. He—he hurt me, Kay!"

"Spare me the sob story," Kay had snapped. "What counts is that I was your lifeline and now, when I ask you to be mine, you look at me as if I'm the devil incarnate and you whimper 'no, I can't!' Is that your idea of how to repay a debt?"

"Kay. Please. Listen to me. What you're asking—"

"What I'm asking for is what you owe me, Ivy. You're always saying I saved your life. Well, now you owe me mine."

It had gone on for hours, Kay talking about what she'd done for Ivy, how Ivy owed her everything, Ivy saying no, no—

In the end, she'd finally given in even though she knew it was wrong, knew she was taking the first step toward breaking her own heart, knew she could not imagine how she would ever give up a baby conceived with a sperm-filled condom, with a syringe, both conveniently tucked inside a little box her stepsister had produced...

"Glyka mou?"

Ivy looked up. Damian smiled as he walked toward her. He was shirtless, barefoot; he wore only denim shorts. His jaw was stubbled because today was Saturday and he hadn't shaved…

Her heart rose into her throat.

How she loved him!

And how cruelly she was deceiving him.

She wore his ring now—a diamond so magnificent it made her breath catch just to look at it. A tiny gold shield that bore his family crest—a lance, a shield and, she now knew, an ancient Minoan bull—dangled from a delicate chain around her neck. Their wedding day was only a week away—and she was still living a lie.

Tears welled in her eyes just as Damian reached her.

"Hey," he said, taking her in his arms, "sweetheart, what's wrong?"

Everything, she thought, everything was wrong! What would he think of her when he knew exactly why she'd been afraid of sex? When he knew the truth about the baby?

"Ivy? *Kardia mou,* tell me what makes you weep."

She couldn't do it. Not yet.

"I'm just—I'm happy, that's all," she whispered, burying her face against his shoulder.

Damian held her close, kissing her hair, her temple, rocking her gently against him…

Aware, in every fiber of his being, she was not telling him the truth.

Yes, his Ivy was happy. He knew it because he was happy, too, though "happy" was far too small a word for what he felt.

He was ecstatic.

Love, commitment, the Big M word had always seemed meant for others. He was not ready to settle down and have children, or even tie himself to one woman.

Then Ivy came along, and all of that changed.

He loved looking up on a Sunday morning to see her biting her lip as she worked a crossword puzzle. Loved the sound of her laughter when a wave caught him and soaked him from head to toe.

Loved the way she fit into his arms when he took her dancing at the little jazz club on the seedy edge of Piraeus, the way she closed her eyes and let the music wash over her.

He loved waking with her in his arms and falling asleep with her in them at night.

That his child was in her womb was icing on the cake.

It wasn't her child, not biologically, and yes, he wished it were, but the other day, when a tiny foot or maybe an elbow had jabbed against his palm, he'd suddenly thought, *Ivy is the reason this precious life exists.*

And he'd imagined his son slipping from her womb, feeding greedily from her breast, and his heart had filled with almost unimaginable joy.

"Glyka mou," he'd whispered, "I am so very happy."

And his Ivy had smiled, brought his mouth down to hers, shown him with her lips, her body, that she was happy, too.

Did she really think he would believe she was weeping in his arms now only because she was happy?

Something was troubling her. Something she'd been keeping from him far too long.

Gently he lifted her in his arms and carried her up the beach, to the dark blue awning of the sprawling cabana he'd had built after he'd inherited Minos and started spending most of his time on the island. He sat her in a lounge chair, went inside the cabana, brought out a box of tissues and blotted her eyes, held one to her nose.

"Blow."

She did. He almost laughed that his elegant Ivy could sound like a honking goose but a man who laughed when his woman wept deserved whatever punishment he got in return.

After a while, her tears stopped.

"Better?"

She nodded.

"Good." Damian squatted in front of her and took her hands in his. "Now, tell me why you weep." He brushed her mouth with his. "The truth, sweetheart. It is time."

Ivy raised her head. "You're right," she said. "It is." She paused. "I—I haven't been honest with you."

Damian nodded. "Go on."

Her face was so pale. He kissed her again, putting his love, his heart, into the kiss.

"Whatever it is," he said softly, "I will still love you."

Would he? She took a steadying breath.

"I've let you think a man—a man hurt me and—and that's the reason I was afraid of sex."

Her words came out in a rush. Damian's smile tilted. "But?"

"But—but it was my fault," she said, her voice so soft it was barely a whisper. "I mean, he did hurt me, but—"

"If someone hurt you, how could it possibly be your fault?"

She told him.

She started at the beginning. The death of her own father. Her mother marrying Kay's widowed father a couple of years later.

"I loved him almost as much as I'd loved my real father," she said. Her voice trembled. "So when he died—when they both died, my mom and my stepfather—"

"Ah, sweetheart. Stop if it hurts you to talk about it."

"You need to know, Damian. I—I need to tell you."

He nodded. "I'm listening."

"It was almost unbearable. Thank God I had—I had Kay."

"Kay." His mouth twisted.

"I was ten. She was fourteen. We'd never been close—the age difference, I guess—but when our parents died…" Ivy swallowed hard. "They put us into foster care. Together. And Kay was—she was—"

"Your lifeline?"

There it was. That same word Kay had used. Ivy nodded. "Yes."

"And?"

"And—and we were in one place that was okay. In another that wasn't. And—and I was accused of—of taking money—"

Damian tugged Ivy from the chaise into his lap. "You don't have to tell me any of this," he said, trying not to let her hear the anger in his voice, the anger of a man imagining a child dropped into a state system, alone, unwanted—

"I hadn't stolen the money, Damian. I don't know who did, but they—they put me back in the Placement center for a while."

God, his heart was going to break. And he knew, without question, who had stolen the money and let Ivy take the blame.

"And then they placed me with—with a man and a

woman. Not Kay. She'd turned eighteen. She left foster care."

"*Ivy.* I love you. There's no need to—"

"I have to tell you so you'll understand why I—why I agreed to carry Kay's baby."

"And mine," he said softly.

Ivy nodded. "Yes. You have to know, Damian."

"I don't," he said gently, and meant it. "But I can see that you have to tell me."

She nodded again, thankful that he understood.

"So," he said, cupping her face, "tell me, and we can put the past behind us."

Could they? When he knew everything? Ivy prayed he was right.

"They placed me with this couple. She didn't pay any attention to me. Well, she did, but—but he—he was kind to me. He said he'd always wanted a daughter. A little girl of his own. He bought me things. A doll. I was old for dolls but nobody had given me anything since—since our parents' deaths and—"

"And you were grateful," Damian said, and wondered at the coldness stealing into his heart.

"Grateful. And happy, even though I didn't see Kay anymore. I understood," she said quickly, seeing the lift of Damian's eyebrows. "I mean, she was busy. Working. She had friends. She was grown up and I…" Her voice trailed away and then she cleared her throat. "My foster father said he knew I was lonely. He began coming into my room to tuck me in. To kiss me good-night. I thought—I thought he was—he was—"

"What did the bastard do to you?"

She stared at Damian. She had seen him angry, even furious, but she had never seen him like this, his eyes black, his mouth thinned, his hands so tight on her shoulders that she knew his fingers must be leaving bruises on her skin.

"He…" *Oh God. Oh God…* "He raped me."

Damian hit the little table where he'd put the tissue box so hard it almost shattered. His arms went around her; he held her tight against him.

"And—and it was all my fault."

"What?"

"My fault, Damian. I didn't realize it until—until I finally found Kay's phone number and called her, and she came to the house where I lived and I told her what had happened and she made me see that I'd provoked it, that I should never have let him tuck me in or kiss me or even buy me that doll and I *knew* that, all along, I knew it was strange but I just thought—I just thought he liked me. Loved me. That he really wanted to be my father, and—"

Damian kissed her.

There was no other way to stop the racing river of pain-filled words except to cover Ivy's mouth with his and kiss her and kiss her and kiss her until, at last, she began to cry, her tears hot and salty against his lips.

"Ivy," he whispered, "*agapimeni,* my darling, my heart, none of it was your fault. Damn Kay for telling you that it was!"

"It was. I should have known—"

"What? That a monster would take a little girl's grief and use it to slake his sick desires?" Damian rocked her in his arms. "Ivy, sweetheart, no one would ever think what happened was your fault. Surely when you reported it—"

"I didn't."

"What?"

"He said—he said, if I told anyone, he'd deny it. And if—if a doctor examined me, he'd say—he'd say he'd caught me with boys in the neighborhood. And since I'd—I'd already been accused of stealing money, they'd believe him, not me. And I—I knew he was right, that nobody would listen to me—"

Damian pounded his fist against the table again. This time, it shattered and collapsed on the sand.

"Who is this man? Tell me his name. I will kill him!"

"Kay took me to live with her. Do you see? She saved me, Damian. She saved me! If she hadn't taken me from him—"

"She did not save you," he said viciously, his accent thickening, his thoughts coming in Greek instead of English. "She used you, *glyka mou*. She told you—you, a child—that you had caused your own rape."

"She made me see my foolishness, Damian."

"And she waited and waited, your bitch of a stepsister, waited until a time came when she could demand repayment," he said through his teeth because now, finally, he understood why Ivy had agreed to bear his child.

"No." Ivy's voice was a broken whisper. "You don't understand. I owed her for saving me."

Damian fought for control when what he really wanted to do was find the beast who'd done this and kill him. And, *Thee mou*, if Kay were alive…

"Ivy," he said, "listen to me. You saved yourself."

"I didn't. If I'd saved myself, I'd never have let what happened happen."

"Sweetheart. You thought this man loved you as a father. Why would you have ever imagined otherwise?

You were a child. Innocent. Lonely. Alone." He paused, framed her face with his hands, made her meet his gaze. "Kay lied to you. It was never, not even remotely, your fault."

Ivy stared at him. "No?" she whispered.

"No. Absolutely not." He drew a breath. "But she'd planted the seed, and she knew it. So, years later, when she wanted something she knew you would not wish to do—"

"Bearing a baby for her," Ivy said, as the tears flowed down her cheeks. "Oh, Damian, I didn't want to! I said no, I couldn't, I couldn't have a child in my womb, feel it kick, see it born and—and give it up—"

"And she said…" He struggled to keep his tone even. "She said, you owed it to her."

"She said she'd saved me once and now—now I had to save her."

Ivy began to sob. Damian folded her into his arms. There was nothing more to say except one phrase, and he repeated it over and over and over, until, finally, her weeping stopped.

"I love you, Ivy," he repeated. "I love you with all my heart."

She drew back and looked at him. "Even after this?"

"Especially after this," he said softly. "Because now I know what true goodness is in your heart, that you would agree to make such a sacrifice for someone you loved."

"Damian. There's—there's more."

His mouth was gentle on hers.

"Later."

"No. No, now. I have to tell you now."

"Later," he said, and kissed her again, and then he

lay her back against the warm sand, under the warm sun, and when he made love to her this time, Ivy wept again.

With happiness.

CHAPTER TWELVE

THEY spent the afternoon on the beach.

Damian had arranged everything. The picnic lunch brought them by Esias. The chilled champagne.

When the sun began its soft pink, purple and violet drop into the sea, Ivy smiled and asked if Damian had arranged for that, too.

"Because the sunset is perfect," she said softly, resting her head on his shoulder as she stood in the curve of his arm, "just like this entire day's been perfect. It's beautiful enough to put a lump in my throat."

"You are what is beautiful, *kardia mou*," he said, drawing her closer. "And I love you with all my heart."

She hesitated. "Even after what I told you?"

"*Neh*. Yes. I told you, especially after that. I only wish it had never happened to you, sweetheart. The ugliness of it. The pain—"

"You took it all away, that first time we made love."

Damian turned her toward him. "Ivy. I want you to promise something to me."

She smiled. "Just ask."

"Never be afraid to share anything with me, *glyka mou*. Your hopes, your dreams..." He ran his thumb lightly over her mouth. "Your darkest secrets," he said quietly. "I will love you, always. Do you understand?"

And, just that quickly, she remembered what she had tried to forget during the long, glorious afternoon.

The final truth.

The last secret.

How would he deal with it? He'd understood why she'd agreed to carry a child of Kay's, but could he understand this?

Not even she understood it. Yes, Kay had been frantic. Yes, there'd been no time to think. And, yes, considering her own plans for the future, her conviction she would never want to make love with a man, that she'd surely never, ever marry, it had made a crazy kind of sense…

"Ivy. Why such a sad look in your beautiful eyes?"

Ivy ran the tip of her tongue over her lips. "There's one last thing I have to tell you, Damian. I tried, hours ago, but—"

"But," he said huskily, "I was more interested in making love than listening."

He smiled. She did, too. Then she rose on her toes and pressed her lips to his.

"Let's go back to our bedroom."

"A fine idea."

"I'll shower, and then—"

"*We'll* shower," he said, with the kind of sexy look that always turned her inside out. "And then we'll have dinner on the terrace in the garden." He took her hands and raised them to his lips. "And you can tell me this last secret so I can kiss you and tell you that whatever it is, it changes nothing."

"I love you so much," Ivy said, her voice breaking. "So much…"

One last, deep kiss. Then they walked to the road, where Damian had parked the Jeep, and drove to what had now become home.

They showered together, and made love, and dried each other off and, inevitably, made love again.

Then they dressed.

Ivy put on a classically long, slender black gown with thin straps. "Look at how my belly shows," she said, laughing, and Damian quickly knelt and put his lips to the bump.

Maybe, she thought, holding her breath as she looked down at him, maybe what she had to tell him would go well.

He rose to his feet and took her hand. "You are so beautiful," he said softly.

She smiled and looked at him in his white jacket and black trousers. "So are you."

He laughed, even blushed. "Men can't be beautiful."

He was wrong. Her Damian *was* beautiful. In face and body. In heart and soul. And yes, he *would* understand this, her last secret.

He had to.

Damian led her down the wide marble stairs, through the oldest part of the palace to a columned terrace in a garden that overlooked the sea.

The table was lit by tall tapers in silver holders. Flowers—white orchids, crimson roses, pale pink tulips—overflowed from a magnificent urn. Champagne stood chilling in a silver bucket and a fat ivory moon sailed over the Aegean…

And standing beside the table, smiling, looking even more stunning than in the past, stood Kay.

Ivy cried out in shock. Damian said a single sharp word. Kay's smile grew brighter.

"Isn't anyone going to say hello?"

"Your Highness." Esias, standing near Kay, all but wrung his hands. "I could not keep the lady out, sir. I am sorry. So sorry—"

Damian dismissed his houseman with a curt nod. His hand tightened on Ivy's but, after a shocked couple of seconds, she tore free of his grasp and ran to her step-sister.

"Ohmygod, Kay! Kay, you're alive!"

"Bright as always, Ivy. That, at least, hasn't changed."

Ivy reached out to hug her but Kay sidestepped, her eyes locked to Damian's.

"And you," she said, "were always a fast worker. I see you didn't waste any time, replacing me."

"Obviously," Damian said, his voice cold, "you didn't die in that car crash."

Kay laughed. "Obviously not."

"Did you have amnesia?" Ivy said. "You must have, otherwise—"

"People have amnesia in soap operas," Kay said. "Not in real life. I went off a cliff into Long Island Sound. Everyone thought I'd drowned."

"They declared you dead," Damian said in that same icy voice.

"Well, I wasn't. I washed ashore a couple of miles away. Carlos's uncle—he's with the government—and a discreet doctor kept the story out of the papers." Her hand went to her face. "I had some bad cuts—it took a lot of plastic surgery—but I'm all healed now." She tilted her head to catch the candlelight. "What do you think, Damian darling? As good as new, or even better?"

"What do you want, Kay?"

"What do I want?" Her smile hardened as she moved slowly across the terrace to where he stood. "Why, I want my life back, of course." She stopped in front of him and lay a hand on his chest. "I want you, darling. A wedding ring. And that delightful little lump I see in my dear sister's belly, as soon as it's born."

Damian caught her wrist and drew her hand to her side.

"Sorry, but you're not getting any of those things." He stepped past her and put his arm around Ivy, who was trembling. "Ivy and I are getting married."

"Ah. You're angry about Carlos. It didn't mean a thing, darling. You're the only one I ever loved."

"You've never loved anyone in your life," he said coldly.

Kay's eyes narrowed. "You don't understand, Damian. I'm back. Whatever little trap my dear sister sprang on you has no meaning now."

Ivy stiffened. "I didn't—"

"Hush, *glyka mou*. There's no need to explain. Kay and I never had marriage plans."

"We certainly did!"

"We did not. *You* had plans, Kay, the first time you told me you were pregnant." Damian's voice turned even more frigid. "It was a lie."

"It wasn't. My doctor—"

"I've seen your doctor. You were never pregnant. And you and I never discussed artificial insemination."

"That's all in the past. I'm pregnant now. I mean, Ivy is. With…" Her eyes flashed to Ivy. "With your child and mine. She did tell you that, Damian, didn't she? That she's carrying your baby? My baby?"

Damian's jaw tightened. "Ivy carries my son." He put his hand on Ivy's round belly. "*Our* son. Hers and mine."

Kay's face paled. "What do you mean? Ivy? What did you—"

"Nothing," Ivy said desperately. "But I will. I will! Kay, you can't just come back after all this time and—and—"

"I can," Kay said fiercely. "I have. And I want what's mine."

"Biology doesn't make for motherhood," Damian snapped. "You were alive, yet you didn't see fit to tell me that you were. You didn't see fit to tell Ivy, even though you knew she was pregnant." His mouth twisted. "You have given up any right to this child."

"I've given up nothing! Not you. Not the baby. And nothing you say or do will change that."

Damian touched Ivy's cheek with a gentle hand. Then he stepped away from her and walked slowly toward Kay.

"I am not a fifteen-year-old girl," he said softly. "I am not a frightened child who will bend to your will. Your lies cannot make me think you are anything more than you are. An evil, selfish woman."

"Ah." Kay laughed. "So, she told you her sad story, hmm? About how the big, bad man molested her?" Her smile vanished; she shot Ivy a look of pure evil. "Liar! Why not tell him the truth? That you were a seductive little bitch—"

"Watch your mouth," Damian snarled.

"A seductive little piece of tail." She whirled toward

Damian. "It's the truth and she knows it. First she seduced my father—"

"No!" Ivy shook her head. "Kay. You know I never—"

"Seduced him. Batted her lashes. Crept into his lap. Told him how much she loved him—"

"I did love him! I was a little girl—"

"And then he died. Her mother died. They put us in foster care and she stole money."

"I didn't steal anything! Kay, I beg you, don't do this!"

"I got out as soon as I hit eighteen. And my dear stepsister lucked out. They put her in another home with a man like my father. And when the poor bastard finally took what she'd been waving under his nose—"

"Paliogyneko!" Damian grabbed Kay's arm and jerked her forward. "Get out! Get the hell out of my home. If I ever see you again, I'll—"

"My God, you bought her story! She told you he raped her. And you believed it!"

"Kay," Ivy pleaded, "stop! We're sisters. I always loved you—"

"Stepsisters. And your supposed love doesn't mean a thing to me." Kay spun toward Damian. "What else did she tell you? That she's been scared of sex ever since?" She threw back her head and laughed. "Look at her, Damian. Think about the life she's led. She moves in a world where people trade in flesh. Where women sell cars by making men get hard-ons. Do you really think my dear stepsister is a sweet portrait of virtue?"

Ivy shook her head. "Damian. Don't listen to her. I've never—"

"You want to know what a good, kind little innocent

my stepsister is?" Kay flashed a vicious smile. "That baby in her belly?"

"Kay. Oh, please, please, please, Kay, don't do this!"

"You remember that charge at Tiffany? That I let you think was mine? It wasn't. I spent it on her. On Ivy. She wanted a necklace. Diamonds. Rubies. I bought it for her."

"Damian. God, she's lying!"

"It was the price for the baby." Kay paused, threw a triumphant look at Ivy, then turned back to Damian. "Because, you see, she's right. I *did* lie, darling. That baby inside her? It's yours, all right…but it's yours and Ivy's."

Ivy swung toward Damian, saw the color leach from his face.

"What?" he said, his voice a husky rasp.

"I found out I couldn't use my own eggs. So I said, Ivy, let me use yours. And she said—"

"Damian. Listen to me. It wasn't like that. It wasn't—"

"I said, how about letting me put my lover's sperm inside you? How about conceiving a baby for me? And she said, is he rich? And I said, yes, he's a royal. And she said, how much can you get out of him? And I said, well, I couldn't come right out and ask for money but I could buy her something she wanted, and she said, how about this necklace at Tiffany? And that was enough until she thought I was dead and she figured, hey, no more middleman. I can collect all the bucks, marry Kay's prince and live the life I've always wanted."

Ivy saw the horror in Damian's face. She turned and ran.

No footsteps came after her.

No footsteps. No Damian. Kay's story was a hideous blend of truth and lies and he'd believed it.

She raced through the vast rooms of the ancient palace, through the entry hall. Esias called to her but she ran past him, out the door, down the steps, along the road that led to the airstrip, her breath sobbing in her throat.

"Ivy!"

She heard the footsteps now. Heard Damian's voice and knew she could not face him. She hadn't told him the final truth for just this reason, because she'd feared what she'd see in his eyes, a look that asked how a woman could agree to conceive a baby and give it up.

"Ivy!"

Weeping, she ran faster. A high-heeled sandal fell off and she kicked away the other one, felt the gravel cutting her flesh and knew the pain of that was nothing compared to the pain in her heart.

"Ivy, damn it…"

Hard arms closed around her.

"No," she shouted. "No, Damian, don't—"

He swung her toward him, his face harsh and angular in the moonlight.

"Ivy," he said—and kissed her.

Kissed her and kissed her, and at first she fought him and then, oh then, she sobbed his name and leaned into him, wound her arms around his neck and kissed him with all the love in her heart.

"*Glyka mou,*" he said, his voice shaky, "where were you going?"

"Away. From here. From you. From all the lies—"

He caught her face in his hands, kissed her again and again.

"I love you," he said, "and you love me. Those are not lies."

"How can you love me now that you know—"

"Don't you remember what I said this afternoon? That you would tell me your last secret and I would tell you I loved you? That I would love you forever?"

"But the baby—"

"Our baby," he said, a smile lighting his face. "Truly our baby, sweetheart, *neh?*"

"Yes. Oh, yes. Our baby, Damian. It's always been ours."

"You did it out of love for Kay."

She nodded. "Yes. No. I thought I did it for her—but I did it for me, too. I was sure I would never marry. Never have sex. Never have children. And I thought, if I do this, if I have this baby, I'll be its aunt. And its mother. In my heart, I'll always be its mother, even if the baby never knows."

"Sweetheart. You're trembling." Damian stripped off his jacket and wrapped her in it. "Come back to the palace."

"No. Not until I've told you everything." Ivy took a deep breath. "So—so I let Kay—I let her do the procedure. And it took. I missed my very next period—" Her voice broke. "And that was when I knew I'd made a terrible mistake, that I would never be able to give away the baby." Her hand went to her belly. "My baby."

"And mine," Damian said softly.

Ivy nodded. "My baby, and yours. I called Kay. I told her. I said she had to tell you the truth. She said it was too late, that we'd made a bargain. I said I would never give up the baby. And then—and then—"

"And then," he said gently, "you thought she'd died."

"Yes."

"So, you waited for me to contact you because you thought I knew all about the baby."

"Not all. I mean, I thought you knew I was carrying your baby but Kay had made it clear she didn't want you to know it was my egg, not hers, that had been fertilized."

"But I didn't contact you."

"No. I assumed it was because you were devastated, losing Kay. That you'd adored her, just the way she'd said you did. And I thought—I thought I owed it to you to let you know the baby was fine, that you were going to be a father, and—and—"

"And?" he said softly.

Ivy shuddered. "And, I hadn't figured out the rest. How to tell you I was the baby's real mother. When to tell you. And then you said you didn't know anything about a baby, that I was up to some kind of awful scam, and I didn't know what to do—"

"Come here," Damian said gruffly, and he gathered her into his arms and kissed her. "Ivy," he whispered, when finally he raised his head, "*glyka mou,* I am so sorry."

"For what?"

"For all you've been through. I love you, *agapimeni.* I love you with all my heart, and I promise to spend the rest of my life making sure you know it. Will you let me?"

Ivy laughed. Or maybe she wept. She couldn't tell anymore because her joy was so complete.

"Only if you let me do the same thing for you," she said, and kissed him.

They made their way back to the palace, arms around each other. At the front steps, Ivy paused.

"Kay?" she said questioningly.

"Gone," Damian said flatly. "She came by boat, or maybe by broom, for all I know, and she's gone back the same way."

"It breaks my heart," Ivy whispered. "To think she hates me enough to have told such lies…" She took a deep breath. "She's still my stepsister. I can't help but hope that someday—"

Damian drew her close. "Anything is possible."

But he knew, even as he said it, that of all the things that had been said on this night, that was the biggest lie of all.

The wedding was on Damian's yacht, anchored just off Minos.

The sun was bright, the sea was wine-dark and the bride, of course, was beautiful.

Some of the models Ivy had worked with for years were there, as was her agent.

There were two best men instead of one. Nicolo Barbieri—Prince Nicolo Barbieri—and Prince Lucas Reyes.

Nicolo was there with his beautiful wife, Aimee, and their adorable baby.

Lucas was alone, by choice.

"Bring a date," Damian had told his pal but Lucas knew better. A man took a woman to a wedding, she got ideas.

Useless ideas, he thought firmly, because as happy as Nicolo was, as happy as Damian was, they could keep the marriage thing for themselves.

Not me, he told himself as he watched Damian kiss his glowing bride, never me.

But never, as everyone knows, is a very, very long time…

0807/06

Mediterranean Men

Let them sweep you off your feet!

Gorgeous Greeks

The Greek Bridegroom by Helen Bianchin
The Greek Tycoon's Mistress by Julia James
Available 20th July 2007

Seductive Spaniards

At the Spaniard's Pleasure by Jacqueline Baird
The Spaniard's Woman by Diana Hamilton
Available 17th August 2007

Irresistible Italians

The Italian's Wife by Lynne Graham
The Italian's Passionate Proposal by Sarah Morgan
Available 21st September 2007

FREE

4 BOOKS AND A SURPRISE GIFT!

We would like to take this opportunity to thank you for reading this Mills & Boon® book by offering you the chance to take FOUR more specially selected titles from the Modern™ series absolutely FREE! We're also making this offer to introduce you to the benefits of the Mills & Boon® Reader Service™—

> ★ **FREE home delivery**
> ★ **FREE gifts and competitions**
> ★ **FREE monthly Newsletter**
> ★ **Books available before they're in the shops**
> ★ **Exclusive Reader Service offers**

Accepting these FREE books and gift places you under no obligation to buy; you may cancel at any time, even after receiving your free shipment. Simply complete your details below and return the entire page to the address below. You don't even need a stamp!

YES! Please send me 4 free Modern books and a surprise gift. I understand that unless you hear from me, I will receive 6 superb new titles every month for just £2.89 each, postage and packing free. I am under no obligation to purchase any books and may cancel my subscription at any time. The free books and gift will be mine to keep in any case.

P7ZEE

Ms/Mrs/Miss/Mr.............................Initials ....

BLOCK CAPITALS PLEASE

Surname ....

Address ....

....

....Postcode ....

Send this whole page to:

The Reader Service, FREEPOST CN81, Croydon, CR9 3WZ

Offer valid in UK only and is not available to current Mills & Boon® Reader Service™subscribers to this series.
Overseas and Eire please write for details. We reserve the right to refuse an application and applicants must be aged 18 years or over. Only one application per household. Terms and prices subject to change without notice. Offer expires 31st October 2007. As a result of this application, you may receive offers from Harlequin Mills & Boon and other carefully selected companies. If you would prefer not to share in this opportunity please write to The Data Manager at PO Box 676, Richmond, TW9 1WU.

Mills & Boon® is a registered trademark owned by Harlequin Mills & Boon Limited.
Modern™ is being used as a trademark. The Mills & Boon® Reader Service™ is being used as a trademark.